DANCE FOR DADDY

SIGGY SHADE

Copyright © 2023 by Siggy Shade

All rights reserved.

No part of this book may be reproduced in any form or by any electronic or mechanical means, including information storage and retrieval systems, without written permission from the author, except for the use of brief quotations in a book review.

Dance for Daddy

SIGGY SHADE

Content Warnings

This book contains graphic sexual content and elements that may be triggering to readers. Please review the list of content warnings to make sure you're comfortable with reading this book before you continue:

Age gap
Arranged marriage
Degradation
Exhibitionism
Public sex
Voyeurism

Chapter One

Declan is driving way too fast.

Again.

And there's a part of me that wants him to crash. Maybe then I'll get out of this ridiculous engagement.

I lean back into the leather seat, breathing hard and fast. My hands curl so tightly into fists that the diamond engagement ring cuts off my circulation.

Sometimes, I resent the world for the sacrifice I'm making to save my family from ruin. I would never cross paths with a man like Declan, let alone agree to become his wife.

He seems to think he's untouchable because his father is a high-ranking member of the Irish mob.

"Slow down," I say for the fourth time. "If you lose your license—"

"Aileen, Aileen, Aileen. When will you ever learn? One of my brothers will get me another." He snickers.

My gaze slides across the BMW's front seat toward the man I'm going to marry next month, and I try not to sigh. Try not to wish I was marrying one of his other brothers or his grandfather because even the leader of the Irish Mob is better than Declan.

His strawberry blond hair is several shades lighter than my mousy brown. He wears it cropped short at the back and sides with lighting bolt patterns shaved from his temples to the nape of his neck. At the top are cornrows that he's arranged into a ponytail.

My gaze travels down to the gold chains hanging around his neck. He thinks he looks like Macklemore or one of the other successful rappers, but it looks more like he's stolen a lord mayor's ceremonial necklace.

I can't dwell on such nasty thoughts. Not when Dad's continual survival rests on me marrying a man I can barely stand.

Declan drives over a zebra crossing, startling a woman with a stroller.

A sharp hiss whistles through my teeth. We have absolutely nothing in common. I'm studying English Lit, and he thinks books are only good to make roaches for spliffs. I don't like drugs, while Declan is always stoned.

He only tolerates me because his father threatened to cut him off if he didn't get married.

The worst part about this is that his father and brothers are so cultured and well-educated. Mr. Macan is ridiculously handsome, sophisticated, and always knows how to conduct himself with grace. Same with the other men in that family. They all hold positions of responsibility within the mob or in local businesses, yet at the age of twenty-two, all Declan wants to be is a fuck boy.

"Where did you say you wanted to go?" he asks.

"Jennifer's," I reply for the third time.

He snorts. "That stripper?"

I bristle, my fingers fiddling with the rim of my glasses. Jennifer and I have been best friends since we met at toddler ballet. She's the only person who kept me sane during this engagement—the only person who doesn't want me subservient and insecure. I'll be damned if he insults her.

"She's an aerobics instructor who combines pole dance fitness, burlesque, and yoga."

"But there's a pole, innit?" He releases the steering wheel and leans across the dashboard for a pack of cigarettes. "Any woman who dances for money is a slag."

Irritation tightens my skin until every inch of it itches. "Fine words for the man who posted a video of himself making it rain over a pair of twerking strippers."

He huffs a laugh. "You saw that? I never pegged you for a stalker."

Shaking my head, I turn my attention back to the street. What's the point of arguing? There's no escaping this arranged marriage. I tell myself that it shouldn't matter if Declan posts videos on social media of himself cavorting with paid models.

I should be grateful he hasn't demanded that I put on lingerie and heels for the camera.

The car drifts to the middle of the road and toward a delivery driver on a bicycle.

I grab the wheel and hiss, "Watch where you're driving."

Declan sniffs. "Those dance lessons won't make a difference. You'll still be a dumpy fuck."

His insult hits straight into my gut, flaring up old insecurities. I've always been the girl that boys over-looked for my taller, thinner, blonder friends. None of that used to matter because there's always someone out there who appreciates you for who you are. I just never expected to marry someone who wanted the complete opposite.

I suck in a deep breath, pull back my shoulders,

and say, "If by boring you mean waiting until we're married before I have sex, then I'll take that as a compliment."

His gaze slides down my tank top and leggings. "You need to lose ten pounds, dress better. Do something with your hair. Wear some fucking heels. Show a bit of cleavage."

"I'll take that under advisement," I say, my words clipped. "May I return the favor and suggest you stop trying to cosplay Vanilla Ice—"

"Right now, the only thing you've got going for you are those tits," he yells.

"Is that why you're cheating?"

The corner of his lips lifts into a smile. "We're not married yet, darlin'."

My hands curl into fists. It takes every ounce of effort to hold back an insult.

I'm not normally such a pushover, but our family is in so much trouble right now that we need to join forces with the mob.

Dad's former business partner disappeared with fifteen million, not only wiping us out but leaving the company owing money to loan sharks. If Declan's father didn't swoop in with a solution that would benefit both families, we would all be out on the street.

Or worse.

If I mess things up with Declan, then his father won't just withdraw his financial support. We'll be in debt to one of the most powerful mobsters in London.

The BMW drives through a narrow road flanked by tall tower blocks. Declan slows down and honks his horn at a bunch of kids playing football in the middle of the street. When they don't move, he revs his engine and makes them scatter.

"Did you have to scare those children?" I ask, my voice sharp.

"This place is a shit hole," Declan mutters.

My nostrils flare. There are many things I dislike about my fiancé. He's selfish, arrogant, and spoiled. And he's most definitely cheating. But the thing that aggravates me the most is his inability to answer questions.

Declan parks outside one of the few two-story buildings on the street. It's a row of storefronts in varying degrees of dilapidation. He reaches for the joint he stashed in his cigarette box.

"What do you say?" he drawls.

I pause, resisting his demand to say thank you. "You know I was going to get a bus before you turned up at the house and insisted on giving me a ride."

Declan offers me a blank stare.

"Because you stopped at Ali's for a smoke and wouldn't let me leave until you were finished, I'm four hours late and I have no idea if Jennifer's going to be in."

"Yeah, well, no woman of mine's going to ride on no public transport." He reaches into the inside pocket of his leather jacket.

Declan is wealthy enough to buy me a second-hand car, but that would mean giving me independence. He seems to think his dad bought me as a pet.

"See you later." I unfasten my seatbelt and open the car door, letting in a blast of exhaust fumes.

"Wait." He grabs my wrist.

Declan extracts a thick stack of fifty-pound notes and waves them like he's shooting one of his dumb videos.

I keep my features even. That has to contain ten-thousand pounds—more than enough to pay my university expenses for the next two years.

Our family used to have that sort of wealth but we were never so ostentatious. Declan thinks his life is a permanent rap video, even though he can't carry a rhyme.

His family tolerates this bullshit because he's the youngest of seven brothers and the only one who grew up without their mother. Even his dad took me to one side at the engagement party and explained that Declan needed a good influence, a nice girl who could lure him away from his irresponsible lifestyle.

What Declan needs is a kick in the teeth.

And a job.

His gray eyes twinkle as he peels two fifty-pound notes from the stack and dangles them in front of my face. "Do you want it, darlin'?"

My throat dries, and I swallow hard. Even a hundred pounds could make a difference to my month.

"I could use that for a cab home," I rasp.

"You know what to do." He taps the side of his cheek.

One kiss in exchange for grocery money. I could even stretch it to a few used books. It's not a big deal. Declan has bribed me into doing worse.

"Come on," he says. "It's not like I'll make you suck my cock."

I glance down at his crotch. Since there's no sign of an erection, I lean across the back seat and place a kiss on his cheek. His stubble feels like sandpaper against my lips, and I force back the urge to grimace. My nostrils fill with the mingled scents of marijuana, stale tobacco, and a sharp citrus aftershave.

Declan grabs my throat, making my breath catch.

"Fat little four-eyed snob," he hisses through his teeth, his gray eyes narrowing into malevolent slits.

"Don't think you're better than me because you're at Uni. If I flashed enough cash, you'd get on your knees and swallow me like a chocolate eclair."

My heart lurches. "Let go, or I'll tell your dad."

"Good luck." He releases my throat with a bitter chuckle. "Dad bought you for me, just like he bought me this car when I crashed the last one."

A shudder runs down my spine at the implication that:

a) he plans on misusing me until I break and

b) I'm replaceable.

I draw away from Declan, but he grabs my wrist again and yanks my hand toward his crotch.

"Stop it" I snap.

"Give me that kiss," he says, his hips rising off the seat.

"No," I say through clenched teeth.

Declan shoves me aside. "Fuck off then, if you don't want my money. But you won't get away with being so snooty when you're my wife."

Panic floods my system, making every limb of my body tremble. What is this? The beginning of something sinister? Images flash through my mind of being trapped with a man prone to violence. What on earth does he plan for me after we're married?

Declan sticks his hand between my legs. "You want it, really."

My glasses slip down my nose, making my vision blur. I scramble out of the car and scream, "I don't want you at all."

He lurches across the passenger seat and barks like a rabid dog.

Tumbling backward, I fall on my ass, and my glasses drop to the paving stones with a clatter. Declan roars with laughter and speeds down the road. As he makes a sharp turn around the corner, the door I left open slams shut.

"Fuck," I say through ragged breaths. Maybe it's time to call Mr. Macan and tell him I can't reform his son.

The only thing stopping me from reaching for my phone is the sound of Jennifer screaming from inside the building.

Chapter Two

My gaze snaps to the dance studio. There's no time to dwell on what just happened with Declan. Not with Jennifer screaming. Anything could be happening to her in this rough neighborhood.

Picking up my glasses, I scramble to my feet and jog toward her building. Adrenaline surges through my veins, making my hand tremble so much that I have to fumble through the contents of my bag to find the pepper spray.

"Jennifer?" I shout.

No answer.

I push the door open and step into Jennifer's empty dance studio. It's more like an oversized living room with a wall of mirrors and a stereo at the side.

Three stripper poles take up half of the wall

opposite, along with a tall stack of stability balls, step platforms, and exercise mats, but not a trace of Jennifer.

I slip on my glasses, restoring my vision to perfect clarity. There's still no sign of my friend.

As I head toward the door that leads to the back room, I hear a choked sob.

"Aileen," she whispers, her voice strained.

"Where are you?"

"Behind the balls," she says through panting breaths.

I rush to the equipment to find her lying on her front, with her head twisted to one side and her left leg bent at an awkward angle. Beneath her prone body lies what's left of the fourth pole.

The can of pepper spray drops to the floor with a loud clang, and I hiss through my teeth. I don't know if she's broken her leg, pulled it out of its joint, or wrecked her spine. Moving her might be catastrophic.

"Shit. Let me call an ambulance."

"Wait," she croaks.

"What?" I reach into the bag and grab my phone.

"Th-there's an important dancing gig tonight with a gentlemen's club," she says, her words tumbling over each other.

DANCE FOR DADDY

"Let me tell them you can't make it after I've called for an ambulance."

"No," she says with a pained moan.

I want to pull the stability balls out of the way and crouch at her side, but what if that makes her injuries worse? I read in a book somewhere that shifting fallen people even an inch can set back their recovery.

"Jennifer, we can talk about it after I've called for help—"

"You've got to listen to me," she says, her voice rising several hysterical octaves. "Gigs like this are once in a lifetime. They're paying me five grand for an hour's work."

My breath hitches, but I push aside the surprise. "There's no way you can dance in your condition—"

"You do it."

I step back, my jaw unhinging. It's one thing to practice dances together as BFFs but another to perform in public. She must have bashed her head if she thinks I could carry out such a highly-paid dancing job.

Jennifer groans. "We're the same size—"

"No, we're not." I dial 999.

"We are," she says from the floor. "I've got longer legs, but we're exactly the same where it matters."

The operator answers. I try to block out

Jennifer's attempts to get me to dance and explain what's happened, but she won't stop talking.

"You've got to do this for me," she says through hiccuping sobs. "A gig like this could pay the rent for two months. We can go halves. That money will tide me over while I'm recovering. I know you could use the cash, too."

I answer the operator's questions, assuring her that Jennifer is breathing and is otherwise in good health. When he tells me the ambulance is on the way, I finally exhale and focus on my friend's ramblings.

"Jen, there's no way I can dance as well as you."

Her hysterical laugh makes the fine hairs on the back of my neck stand on end.

"Are you kidding?" She says. "We've danced together since before nursery school. You've always been as good as me. And look how well you do in pole dance fitness."

I rub the back of my neck. "They ordered a leggy blonde. They'll freak when they see me."

"Aileen," she growls. "You already know the routine. It's the one you helped me perfect."

That's the frustrated tone of voice she uses whenever I let one of Declan's insults get through my defenses. The same tone that always boosts my confidence.

My stomach twists into nauseating knots. How can I be so wrapped up in my insecurities when my best friend is lying broken on the floor and potentially unable to earn a living?

Jennifer supported me through a shit-load of trouble. She offered me a place to stay when we thought Dad would lose the house and gave me a shoulder to cry on when Mr. Macan offered to bail us out in exchange for me marrying Declan.

Guilt wraps around my chest and squeezes out all my air. Why, when she's at her lowest, could I possibly refuse her request?

Sucking in a deep breath, I push my insecurities to the pit of my stomach.

"Focus on getting better," I say. "I'll do your gig and give you a hundred percent."

"We'll split it," she replies, her voice less strained.

"You're going to need all the help you can get for the next few weeks. Just tell me where I'm going and what you need me to wear."

Jennifer stutters out an address and tells me that the costume is already hanging up in the back room, along with a pair of stilettos in our size.

I had no idea this gentlemen's club would be on the outskirts of London. It's too late in the day to reach the gig via public transport, but there isn't enough money to get a taxi.

Dread hits my gut like a wrecking ball. At times like this, I wish I'd swallowed my pride, taken the fifty-pound note, and allowed Declan to have his little rant.

The studio's door opens, and a pair of male paramedics enter, holding oversized kit bags. As they head toward the stability balls, I step backward to give them space.

"Aileen?" Jennifer says.

I gulp. "Yes?"

"If you don't start getting changed right now, you'll be late. Someone from the gentlemen's club will pick you up in an hour."

Clutching my stomach, I groan, even though there's a tiny part of me that feels my heart race.

Shit.

It's really happening.

I'm going to dance burlesque for a bunch of paying gentlemen.

Chapter Three

I lean back in the cream leather seats of the Bentley, my heart beating hard enough to drown out the sound of the air conditioning.

This is unbelievable.

When Jennifer told me the gentlemen's club would bring a car, I thought she meant an Uber or even a black cab, but this is beyond my expectations.

She was right about one thing: we're exactly the same dress size. It's unbelievable, considering she has a perfect body while I'm... I shake my head. If I dwell on Declan's taunts, anything left of my confidence will crumble.

I roll my shoulders, smooth down the black leather pencil skirt, and slide my finger down the neckline of the matching top.

It's butter-soft and dips down to where the underwires of my corset meet. I've never worn anything so flattering. The two-piece complements my hourglass figure and tapers down past the knees. I have no idea how Jennifer can afford anything so classy. Perhaps she's had more than one gig with the gentlemen's club.

Before I know it, the driver takes an exit down a dark country road, and I catch the first glimpse of a limestone mansion lit up by flood lights that shimmer across a vast lake.

My heart skips a beat.

It looks like a miniature Buckingham Palace.

This can't be the gentlemen's club.

Minutes later, we're pulling into the front of a grand entrance way of white, marble columns, where a butler in a black frock coat stands before a set of huge double doors.

He steps forward, opens the door, and offers me a gloved hand. "Miss Demeanor, I presume?"

My pulse quickens. Is that Jennifer's stage name? Shit.

I clear my throat. "Yes?"

"Welcome to Pedra-Moura. Our members look forward to tonight's performance."

"Thank you," I croak and take his hand.

After thanking the driver, I follow the butler through the doors, my borrowed stilettos click-clacking on the black-and-white-tiled hallway. My whole house could fit into this space. It's even twice the size of the entrance hall in Declan's mansion but four times more intimidating.

Mr. Macan is one of those fathers who insists on making his sons and their families live under his roof, but even his house isn't nearly as grand.

I hurry past portraits of men in suits from different eras within the past century, and into a narrower hallway where the lights aren't so bright. Some of the tension in my shoulders relax at the change in splendor, and we stop at a door with a brass plaque that says DRESSING ROOM.

"The master of ceremonies will call you out in five minutes," the butler says before turning on his heel.

Already? A jolt of panic squeezes my heart. I push open the door and step into a white dressing room covered with floor-to-ceiling mirrors.

The woman in the reflection is confident and curvaceous. It takes a moment to realize it's me because I'm wearing Jennifer's wig with a mask obscuring the bottom half of my face. The corset beneath the leather two-piece cinches in my waist, giving me the kind of extreme hourglass from the 1950s.

"Bloody hell," I whisper, my bag dropping to the floor with a soft thud.

My cleavage looks incredible. I'm a 34E but always wear minimizer bras. This corset lifts and separates my boobs and accentuates my hips. I look like a pin-up girl.

A knock sounds on a side door, making my pulse quicken.

"Come in?" I rasp.

It opens, letting in the sound of strip-tease music, along with a man dressed as a ringmaster with a top hat and red velvet frock coat. This has to be the Master of Ceremonies.

"Miss Demeanor, you're late," he says, his voice sharp with a reprimand.

"Sorry," I stutter. "I was—"

"Never mind that." He beckons me over. "Come with me. You need to be in place before the current act ends."

As the MC disappears behind the door, I hurry across the dressing room and into an even narrower hallway than the one from before. The music echoes through its plaster walls, giving it the feeling of a secret passage.

I breathe hard, my heart thrashing against my ribcage, trying to find a way to escape.

"Calm down," I whisper under my breath.

DANCE FOR DADDY

"You've done this routine with Jennifer a thousand times."

My heartbeat quickens again at the sight of the MC standing by the door at the end of the hallway. I suck in a deep breath, filling my lungs with so much air that they push against my heart. That's when I remind myself of three facts:

One, I'm unrecognizable with this wig and mask.

Two, Jennifer needs that five grand now more than ever.

Three, without my glasses, I can barely see the gentlemen's expressions.

I release the air in my lungs, my heart calming to a steady beat. When the MC opens a door that leads to a massive room illuminated by purple spotlights, my jaw drops.

A platform the size of Jennifer's entire dance studio takes up the middle and around it are rows of men sitting in leather armchairs. Most of them wear black tuxedos, but some are dressed in white. Only a few of them wear masks. The rest don't because they're drinking.

Shit.

There has to be a hundred men.

"Wait here." The MC places a hand on my shoulder.

It's a good thing I have a few minutes before my act starts because my legs have turned to jelly.

The woman onstage has bubble-gum pink hair and is naked, save for a pair of ostrich-feather fans she sweeps over her essentials. She's voluptuous, with thick thighs and a dimpled ass.

Each time the audience catches a glimpse of her boobs, they cheer. There's even a quartet of men throwing £50 notes onto the stage, enticing her to slip up as she gathers the money.

I lean forward, warmth gathering between my thighs. She's so graceful and alluring that even I'm entranced.

Seeing her dance with so much confidence lifts a weight off my shoulders. A woman like her wouldn't shrivel under the weight of Declan's rejections. She would throw her head back and laugh.

"Why can't I be like her?"

I shake my head. These few months have been stressful. There were times when I thought Dad would collapse under the strain of losing everything. Stress has twisted my mind into a myriad of knots, and I let Declan's liquid barbs soak into my skin like poison.

No more.

When the music stops, the room fills with applause. The feather dancer curtsies prettily for the gentlemen, closes her fan, and picks up the rest of the money.

Raucous cheers and wolf whistles ring through my ears, making my pulse quicken with excitement. Sending the feather dancer a silent word of thanks, I straighten and pull back my shoulders.

It no longer matters that my fiancé is a piece of shit who masks his insecurities with body shaming. People come in all shapes and sizes—all equally as beautiful and worthy of love. I feel crazy for not thinking about that until now.

By the end of tonight, I'll have the confidence I need to put Declan in his place.

Chapter Four

A second later, the pulse between my ears pounds so loud that it drowns out the MC's introduction, and every butterfly in my stomach decides now is the time to riot.

I walk to the stage on wooden legs, trying to channel my dwindling confidence. What on earth do I think I'm doing? I have never danced for an audience. Hell, I can't even speak in public.

When the music starts and the MC gives me an encouraging pat on the shoulder, my butterflies drift back to the lining of my stomach, leaving me with a strange sense of calm.

It's time to push aside my nerves. Jennifer's in a hospital bed, probably fretting about how she's going to pay the rent when she can barely stand on two feet.

I've got to do whatever it takes to earn that five grand.

With a dramatic swing of my hips, I step forward in time with the music. The corset is so cinched at the waist that any movement accentuates my hourglass.

Thanks to hours of analyzing burlesque artists like Dita Von Teese, I hold my head up high and mimic her confident expressions, exaggerated poses, and shoulder shimmies.

I trace my fingers over my blouse's low neckline and toward the corset's front fastenings. A few of the gentlemen lean forward, their chests rising and falling with rapid breaths. Instead of opening the garment, I drop my hands back on my hips, and one of the men slumps back, disappointed.

A part of me preens under their admiring gazes.

How I wish Declan could see this.

A tall man walks into my line of sight, dressed differently from the others. He wears a burgundy velvet jacket with a black bowtie and black pants that accentuate his athletic frame.

I can't see much of his features under his burgundy silk mask except for a pair of piercing blue eyes, but that doesn't stop the butterflies in my stomach from fluttering.

DANCE FOR DADDY

Maybe it's because I'm nervous, but he seems more imposing than his peers.

As I run my gloved hands over my curves, he gives me a slow, approving nod that's perfectly timed to the music. My breath catches, and I have to force myself to calm. This isn't some kind of special connection. He's only looking at me because I'm up on stage.

It takes every effort to tear my gaze away from Mr. Burgundy, but the music changes, indicating that it's time to take off the leather gloves. Since I'm still wearing the lacy mask, I can't pull them with my teeth, so it takes every ounce of concentration to synchronize their removal with the melody.

When the first glove comes off and leaves my hand bare, a few of the gentlemen whistle. The MC hovers close, and I toss the glove at him, followed by the other.

At least I know there's someone around to safeguard Jennifer's costume.

Arching out my arm with as much grace as I can muster, I curl my fingers the way Jennifer and I practiced from watching the movements of classical Indian dancers.

Out of the corner of my eye, I see Mr. Burgundy call someone over from the other side of the room.

When the butler arrives and leans in for a conversation, I tell myself to focus on the dance.

As I toe off my shoes, revealing my stockinged feet, one of the men wolf whistles, and my heart soars.

It's crazy. Before Dad and Mr. Macan arranged this marriage, I would have scoffed at the thought of basking under the male gaze. But Declan's constant stream of complaints has washed away any sense of self-worth.

There's a natural pause in the music where I swing the dressage whip, creating a high-pitched sound that makes some of the men sitting opposite draw back with a wince.

That's the sleight of hand Jennifer and I formulated to slip off the leather blouse. I hold it up between my thumb and forefinger, and the men burst into applause.

My pulse quickens. I nearly miss the beat.

Wow.

They really love this dance.

The MC sweeps forward and gathers up my blouse, leaving me rolling my shoulders to the saxophone solo. Some of the gentlemen rise from their seats, obscuring my view of Mr. Burgundy.

It's the cups. They're a size too small and barely constrain my boobs.

The music fades to a rapid beat. I shake my shimmy and move with exaggerated side steps to the opposite end of the stage to entertain a different part of the audience.

Practically every man in the front rises off their seat, and my stomach flips like a crepe. I had better not spill out of this bra.

My gaze falls on a man wearing a white tuxedo jacket, sitting in front with a companion in black. He brings a glass of liquid to his lips and watches me with the concentration of a predator.

Mr. White Tuxedo licks his lips, and the pulse between my legs quickens.

I force my gaze away from him and toward the rest of the audience, only to find Mr. Burgundy has moved to the other side of the stage to get a better look.

My heart flip-flops.

Mr. Burgundy is really paying attention.

A crescendo of violins returns, and I reach behind my back with both hands and make a forward bend with a cute hip roll.

Removing the skirt from this angle is easier, and I pull apart the velcro to transform the garment into a single strip of leather. Gyrating to the music, I hold it in front of my hips for the next few beats. Cheers fill the other side of the stage, where I'm treating the gentlemen to a perfect view of my ass.

All the men in front lean forward, some of them seeming to hold their breath. Excitement pools low in my belly, and the muscles between my legs clench.

Fuck, the power I hold over these men is exhilarating.

My gaze drifts to Mr. Burgundy, the only man in the room not reacting. For a split second, I swear that he winks. I can't linger on him for too long, because the music changes once more.

I glance offstage and give the MC a nod. He strides in and takes my skirt to the applause of the men sitting in front.

Now, I'm standing in a flesh-colored corset adorned with black lace and satin-covered bones. Six garter belts hang down from its sides, holding up a pair of sheer stockings. I should be scandalized that I'm prancing half-naked in front of strange men, but I don't give a shit.

Cheers ring through my ears, making my nipples tighten and rub against the lace cups. The pulse between my legs pounds harder than the drums.

A tiny kernel in the back of my mind still can't believe it's me making these gentlemen excited. Maybe burlesque is where Jennifer gets her extraordinary confidence because I'm starting to feel like a goddess.

I sashay across the stage to dance for a new part of the audience, expecting Mr. Burgundy to follow. When he doesn't, my heart sinks, but all that changes when my gaze falls on the man in the white tuxedo.

He presses the heel of his hand into his crotch, looking like he's trying to stave off an erection.

My tongue darts out to lick my lips.

This is going to be interesting.

Unhooking the metal clips at the front of my corset, I roll my hips like a belly dancer. It's another distraction technique so the audience doesn't notice my fumbling.

Mr. White Tuxedo tracks my hips' movement with his gaze. His eyes burn with a hunger that makes my pussy heat. Any other time, I might cringe, but here on this stage, I'm the one in charge.

As he rises from his seat, my heart kicks up several notches. What on earth is he going to do? I'm so preoccupied with his odd behavior that I barely notice the roar of the crowd.

The MC comes onstage to take my corset, leaving me standing in a lace bra and matching knickers. Unlike my fiancé, these gentlemen don't mind that my belly is rounded.

Holding onto the pole, I swing around it the way Jennifer taught us in fitness classes. When my feet reach the ground, I arch backward and pull off my bra.

The room shakes with thunderous applause, making me jolt. I straighten, my breasts bouncing. The only thing keeping me decent is a pair of leather pasties attached to tiny handcuffs.

Mr. White's jaw drops.

My lips curl into a smile.

A drumroll starts, my cue to lean forward and swing the metal chains in perfect circles.

Mr. White beckons at me to come closer and drops a stack of fifty-pound notes on the stage. I count at least a thousand pounds.

As my gaze travels upward, I find he's taken out his cock.

Now, it's my turn to gasp.

It's long and thick, with a bulbous head that already glistens with precum.

Fuck.

Sensation rushes to my pussy, and I almost lose the rhythm of my steps. Mr. White might be a creep, but he knows how to tease his dick.

Back and forth, he times his strokes to the music, his cock lengthening and thickening. I glance around the audience, trying to gauge their reactions, but a few of them are also touching their cocks.

Damn.

As I meet Mr. White's eyes, he grins and beckons me closer.

A jolt of excitement strikes my heart. It would be so easy to shimmy over and collect that cash but this situation reminds me too much of Declan. What if Mr. White grabs me? What if he forces me to suck him to completion?

The money is tempting, but picking it up feels like regressing into Declan's insecure and unwanted fiancée. I wag my finger at him and gyrate around the pole.

Mr. White continues stroking his cock, and I grind my pussy against the pole's hard metal. Part of me wants to see how far he'll take it—if he would really make himself cum across the stage.

I glance around for Mr. Burgundy, somehow feeling disloyal for my fascination with Mr. White Tuxedo. Since he's nowhere in sight, I continue rubbing my clit against the pole.

There's a drumroll, and White Tuxedo quickens his movements, turning his thick cockhead a delicious shade of purple. I lose track of the routine, my hips gyrating in time with his hand.

Somewhere out of the corner of my eye, I see

other gentlemen rise with their cocks in their hands. Fuck. There's a crowd of men stroking themselves over the way I'm humping a metal pole.

The pulse behind my clit beats faster than the drums, and pressure builds up around my core. I'm so wet, so close, with only the tiniest scrap of fabric separating my bare pussy from the metal.

I really shouldn't be doing something so indecent.

Good girls don't masturbate in public—especially not when wearing a lace thong and a pair of pasties over their nipples. Especially not in front of a hundred men. And especially not when so many of them are stroking their erections.

Blood roars in my ears, muffling the strains of the music. My gaze darts around, taking in the varying shapes and sizes and shades. Long and slender, short and thick, lengthy with impressive girth. There are all manner of cock heads from pale to pink to red to purpling.

All of them getting off at the sight of me taking my pleasure.

My pussy floods with heat, and the pressure building behind my clit is at breaking point. I'm so swollen and wet and needy that I feel every fiber of my lace thong.

The pole I'm using as a rubbing post will need a thorough cleaning.

I turn back to White Tuxedo, who stares at me through blazing eyes, and briefly wonder if Mr. Burgundy is as well endowed. His strokes quicken, his chest rises and falls with rapid breaths, then his cock erupts streams of white cum.

The pressure behind my clit implodes, and an orgasm sweeps through my system, making my knees buckle. I cling onto the pole with both hands, my hips convulsing against its metal shaft.

My eyes roll toward the ceiling, filling my vision with red lights. Every nerve in my body thrums with electricity—I've never had such a powerful climax. As my orgasm intensifies, I catch a flash of movement. Some of the men in front try to mount the stage.

Fuck.

I release the pole and stagger backward, only to bump into the MC.

"Gentlemen," he shouts over the fading music. "Stand back, allow the young lady safe passage, and let's not forget the club's rules of engagement."

I don't wait to see if the men draw back. I don't even bother to pick up the money they left on the stage. Holding down my breasts with my forearm, I sprint to the edge of the platform.

Applause and wolf whistles punctuate my strides, but I'm not in the mood to bask. I rush down the stairs and through the door marked EXIT, not stopping until I reach the dressing room.

When I fling the door open and step inside, I stare into the smiling blue eyes of Mr. Burgundy.

Chapter Five

I stagger backward, nearly falling on my ass when Mr. Burgundy wraps an arm around my waist and holds me steady. My heart pounds harder than the drum solo echoing down the hallway, and I swallow back a yelp.

Up close, he's even more imposing. Six foot four with broad shoulders and the type of athletic build one can only get from rigorous sessions at the gym.

I can smell his cologne through the mask. It's cedar and leather and spice. Sensation ripples through my pussy, partially from being in the presence of this mysteriously hot man and partially from the aftershocks of my interrupted orgasm.

Mr. Burgundy releases his arm from around my waist and steps back into the dressing room, leaving me feeling the loss of his touch.

The corners of his eyes crinkle. "Forgive my forwardness, but I wanted to be the first to make my approach."

My brow furrows, and I wait for him to elaborate.

"Your routine was exquisite. Unfortunately, I missed the end of it to request a private dance."

I step back, my ass hitting the wooden door. "Private?" I gulp, already not trusting myself with such a powerful-looking man. "No, thank you, I don't—"

"Five thousand," he says.

My jaw drops, and I'm glad my mouth is hidden by the mask.

Fuck. Five grand on top of the five I'm earning for tonight's dance would make such a difference. With that sort of money, I could rent a studio at the university's hall of residence, and never have to cross paths with Declan. With that sort of money, I would be free.

Only for a little while. It would take an eight-figure sum to free me of my obligation to the Macan family. That, or a miracle.

I meet Mr. Burgundy's expectant gaze and grimace. If I'm honest with myself, I'd do that private dance for free, just so this powerful man could look at me like I'm special.

My shoulders sag. What's the point? One night of self-confidence isn't going to change the fact that I'll have to marry the world's biggest asshole. I've gotten away with dancing in public so far. Alone time with someone so tempting might lead to trouble with the Macan family.

"I appreciate the offer," I murmur, "But—"

"Ten thousand." He draws closer. "And I promise not to touch."

Ten minutes later, I'm fully dressed again and stepping into a beautiful suite of cerulean walls, mahogany furniture, and silver-framed pictures. A fat roll of fifties sits in my handbag, courtesy of the butler, and I'm about to receive two more of the same from Mr. Burgundy.

The man disappears through a door, leaving my gaze darting to an antique four-poster bed. My heart beats a rapid tempo, and I shuffle on my feet, trying to find a stereo or some other device to hook up my phone to play music.

Sweat breaks out across my palms, and I dab them on the sides of my leather skirt. There's no point in feeling jittery. I already agreed to dance with the man for money.

"Is it alright if I make myself comfortable?" he asks from the other room.

"Sure," I rasp.

He steps out in his shirtsleeves, holding two thick stacks of fifties. The pulse behind my clit quickens. I can't tell if that's because of the money or because of how the white fabric stretches over his defined biceps and pecs.

I stand transfixed, watching him place the money on a dresser and unbutton his cuffs, revealing muscular forearms covered in light-brown hair. His skin is a little paler than I imagined, with a complexion closer to my fiancé's than mine.

Shaking off the thoughts of that smug little bastard, I cross the room and take the bundles. "When would you like me to start?"

"Anytime," he says in a deep drawl. The tone is so suggestive and laden with so much innuendo that my pussy clenches.

It's just a dance, I tell myself and stuff the money into my bag. This isn't a hookup or anything sordid. I'm doing this to help Jennifer and to get a break from Declan. I pull out my phone and fumble through the security screen.

"Let me put on some music," I mutter.

Jennifer has a cool-down routine that involves lots of back arches, hip rolls, and stretching tense muscles with sexy poses. I've performed it so many times that the movements are embedded in my muscle memory.

Mr. Burgundy rests on a cushioned bench at the foot of the four-poster. He releases the top button of his shirt and works his way down its front placket. It takes every ounce of willpower not to stare, so I focus on finding the perfect tune.

"What happened to the other Miss Demeanor?" He leans forward with his fingers steepled, his forearms resting on his muscular thighs

My gaze snaps up from the screen and lands on his defined chest and abs. Did he ever pay Jennifer for a private dance? I snap out of my preoccupation and form an answer to his question that doesn't get either of us into trouble.

"She broke her leg today and asked me to step in." Tapping on the music app, I play Jennifer's cooldown track and set the phone on the dresser.

The music starts, a slow double bass that resonates through my bones. I hold the kind of pose Jennifer makes us practice in the mirror. Right foot forward to create the illusion of slender legs, and left hip cocked to the side to accentuate my curves.

His gaze tracks the moment before bouncing back to my eyes. "You're her partner?"

There's something in the way he says that word

that implies he thinks I'm Jennifer's lover. I shake my head, somehow wanting Mr. Burgundy to know that I very much like men.

I swing my left arm in an arc, making sure to jut my hip.

"We're just friends."

I swing my right arm, bend into a crouch, push out my behind, and roll my body up to standing.

"Do you have a stage name?" he asks, his eyes on my ass.

"I'm not a professional," I reply with a nervous giggle. "This is my first time."

"But you dance so well."

His voice is warm and teasing and sends a tingle across my skin. I raise my arms above my head and bump my hips to the beat. The part of me that believes in fairytales wants to think he's got plans to see me again. The part of me that's firmly entrenched in reality reminds me of the truth.

"Hopefully this performance won't be your last," he says.

"Tonight's a one-off," I say above the clarinet. "I have a fiancé."

The moment I say those words, my chest deflates with a pang of regret. I turn back to Mr. Burgundy, wishing I didn't have to be faithful to Declan.

A medley of trumpets has me shouldering off the leather blouse, and I toss it to the side with a pop of my hips. Bending forward, I switch my shoulders back and forth, making my boobs jiggle in their lace cups.

Mr. Burgundy sits forward in his seat and groans. "Don't you thrive on the attention of an appreciative room of men?"

I roll my hips and bite back a moan at the implication that he finds me attractive. Of course, he does, otherwise, he wouldn't have rushed out of the room to be the first to pay me for a private dance.

"Don't tell me you didn't find it exciting," he says, his voice more insistent as though he demands an answer.

"Sure, it was. But I'm loyal to my fiancé." I pull back my shoulders and slink toward him in time to the beat.

This is the perfect opportunity to release the velcro of my skirt. I let the leather fabric slide down my thighs to the wooden floor.

He rubs his chin, his gaze raking up and down my legs. The gesture is so casual, but his eyes meet mine with an intensity that delivers a jolt of arousal to my pussy and makes me miss a step.

"Yet you were tempted by the offer of ten thousand pounds," he says, his voice measured. "That says your fiancé isn't doing his job of taking care of you."

My throat tightens, and an ache travels deep into my bones. His tone of voice suggests that he's not only talking about the money, and he would be right. I want his muscular body pinning me to the bed while those large hands explore every inch of my flesh.

This man isn't just handsome, he's astute. But his interest in me is a little more than unnerving. Despite my newfound confidence, he already knows I'm neglected. Declan could make my life comfortable in an instant, yet he gets off on seeing me struggle.

Mr. Burgundy leans back to make eye contact. "Tell me something, Miss Demeanor."

"Yes?" I focus on my steps.

"Do you intend to keep the mask on during your routine?"

"Of course."

"I'm aching to see your face," he says. "And a lot more."

My step falters. "But I'm not—"

"I promise not to touch," he says, the corners of his eyes crinkling. "You can even tie my arms to the back of the chair."

The music changes, turning slow and sultry. I

DANCE FOR DADDY

arch my back, holding the stretch for several beats—enough time to consider his proposal. It's one thing to fill in for Jennifer but quite another to accept money for a private dance.

But I can't show my face.

Not when I'm about to marry into the most powerful family within the Irish mob.

What if Mr. Burgundy is also connected? What if I bump into him at a later date, and he recognizes my face? Mr. Macan might decide to withdraw his financial support and the family will be back where we started.

No, it will be worse.

Declan would take delight in making me suffer for dancing in public. He might even force me to perform in one of his stupid videos for laughs.

I meet Mr. Burgundy's burning gaze and sigh. "Look, I'm flattered, but I'm only here just as a favor for my friend."

He squeezes his eyes shut and inhales a deep breath that inflates his pecs. I'm so mesmerized by the way the muscles of his six-pack deepen that I forget my steps.

"It's been years since I've found a woman enticing," he says. "You're like a young Elizabeth Taylor, only twice as alluring."

I bite down on my bottom lip. Surely he's exaggerating. However, the money he just paid me suggests he might be telling the truth.

"What if I added another five grand to the deal and took off my mask?" he asks. "If you're worried about your identity, you'll have mine. Call it a mutually assured destruction."

My brows draw together. "I don't think—"

He pulls off his mask, revealing the chiseled features of a man in his early forties with cheekbones sharp enough to slice throats.

Fuck.

That's Angus Macan.

Declan's dad.

Chapter Six

"Mr. Macan!"

The words slip from my mouth, and I cringe. Now, he's going to wonder how I know him. Declan's dad might be a high-ranking member of the Irish mob, but he keeps a low profile.

He rises from his seat, his brows pulling into a frown. "How do you know my name?"

I step backward, my pulse beating faster than the tempo of the song. How the hell am I going to escape this situation with my secret intact?

The moment he discovers his future daughter-in-law is a stripper, he'll call off the entire engagement. The mob is rumored to value the sanctity of marriage, and they'll see something like this as an affront. It won't be just me who suffers. Shit. Mr.

Macan will call off the arrangement. Then Dad will owe the loan sharks an unholy amount of money.

All because I got drunk on a little bit of power and wanted to bask in the attention of a man I found handsome.

"Answer my question," he says in a voice of steel.

Fuck. I need to leave. Leave right now before I destroy what's left of my family.

Turning around, I rush to the door in my heels, but he's too fast. He grabs my arm, spins me around, and pins me to the wall with his larger body.

He's surprisingly gentle for a man rumored to have wiped out the Fian gang, but I'm not stupid enough to think I'm immune to his wrath.

"Who sent you?" he growls into my ear, the heat of his anger burning hot enough to make me break into a sweat.

"N-nobody," I blurt.

"Someone out there knows my weakness for curvaceous little brunettes and knows the exact type that would make me drop my guard. Now, you're going to tell me everything."

The scrutiny in his eyes is like a brand, burning holes into my veneer of confidence until I jerk my head to the side. "Please," I whisper. "Everything I said earlier was the truth. My friend had an accident—"

DANCE FOR DADDY

He yanks down my mask and hisses a sharp breath. Then he snatches away his hand and steps back.

"Aileen Walsh."

It's not a question. He recognizes me through the heavy makeup and Jennifer's wig.

"Yes, sir." I dip my head, my shoulders curling, and draw my hands to my chest.

"Why would my son's fiancée take off her clothes in public?"

"I was standing in for my friend—"

"Why would you accept money for a private dance?"

Squeezing my eyes shut, I wait for him to strike.

Declan would grab my throat, hiss a barrage of insults, and toss me to the floor. He'd probably use this as an opportunity to say something denigrating.

Mr. Macan draws back, his footsteps receding, and turns off the music.

His lack of action makes my heart gallop around my chest like an out-of-control horse with its mane on fire. I'm about to lose everything. Everything I ever endured for the sake of the family is about to go up in flames. I squeeze my eyes shut, forcing myself to stay calm. There has to be something in this situation I can salvage.

"Aileen, I asked you a question, and I expect a

57

reply," he says, sounding less murderous but no less insistent. "Why would you accept a private dance when you're engaged to my son?"

My head snaps up. "You said it yourself. My fiancé doesn't take care of my needs. He thrives on making me miserable."

His eyes harden. "Explain."

"I'm the opposite of what he wants. He only tolerates this engagement because you threatened to cut him off."

"I see," he says, his words tight.

Mr. Macan isn't throttling me, which is a good sign, so I take the opportunity to speak up. "The last thing Declan said after calling me a fat little snob was something about humbling me after we're married."

"Have you told your parents?"

My shoulders sag, and I drop my gaze to my shoes. "They need this alliance to work."

As Mr. Macan's footsteps draw close, my insides tighten into knots. I'm supposed to be Declan's calming influence. The woman who inspires him to be a better man. Instead, I'm standing half-naked in a room with an older man, just after having climaxed on a public stage.

"Aileen."

I flinch.

"Look at me."

Ignoring the tent in his pants, I force my gaze up his tight abs, past a sculpted chest that rises and falls with rapid breaths, and to a strong jaw.

"You still owe me that dance," he rasps.

"But Declan—"

"We'll work something out." His lips curl into a half smile. "Now, will you continue?"

I bite down on my bottom lip, my heart still pounding. If Declan discovers what I've done... Fuck him. If I have to watch that bastard cavort with hired models on social media, I sure as hell can dance for his dad.

"Alright." I place my hand on his chest, my breath catching when I feel his rapid heartbeat. "But you'll have to go back to your seat."

His half-smile widens into a grin that makes my heart flip. "Good girl."

I have no clue why such simple words would send a bolt of arousal straight to my pussy, but I have to clench my thighs together to stop them from trembling.

Mr. Macan returns to the end of the four-poster and lowers himself on the seat, while I return to my phone and find another track.

The music starts, with a slow horn melody interspersed by staccato drums. I slink toward Mr. Macan in time to the beat, my pussy throbbing. This is more arousing than what I did with the pole. I'm performing for one of the most powerful men I know—the only person who intimidates my fiancé.

His gaze rakes up and down my form. The stare is so intense it almost feels like a caress.

"My son is an idiot," he says, his voice breathy. "You are so unutterably beautiful."

My heart somersaults.

The same words could be said for him. Mr. Macan is the epitome of masculine beauty, athletic, tall, and chiseled. I never dared look him in the eyes the few times we met because of his fierce reputation.

Right now, he's Mr. Burgundy, the man who couldn't take his eyes off me onstage.

I raise my hands above my head and swing my hips into a low crouch, and my gaze drops to the erection bulging through his tuxedo pants. It's longer and thicker than Mr. White Tuxedo's and I can't help but wonder if Mr. Macan will pull it out.

"See something you like?" he asks in a deep drawl.

"Maybe." I rise, place my hands on my waist, and roll my hips.

Mr. Macan's gaze tracks the movement for a few beats before traveling up the front of my corset and settling on my cleavage. He breathes through parted lips, his fingers curling into fists.

My skin tingles with the need to have those hands on my thighs, my breasts, between my legs. The power I have over this man is intoxicating.

The music changes. I turn around and walk to the other end of the room, exaggerating the movement, then pause with a swivel of my hip to glance over my shoulder. Then I give my ass a little spank.

When Mr. Macan rises off the seat, my core clenches with anticipation. He's breathing so hard and fast that he looks fit to rush forward as the gentlemen did earlier.

Part of me wants him to pin me against the wall again, only this time, I won't cower. This time, my hand will do more than touch his chest.

Rolling my shoulders, I stretch out an arm and run my fingers over my skin. This move is designed to arouse, and I swear I hear Mr. Macan growl. I should back away and do something less risqué like a side shuffle, but I run my hands down the curve of my breasts, over my belly, and down my thighs.

He advances on me, each step making my heart beat harder.

Common sense screams at me to stop, to remind him to return to his seat, but the bolt of arousal shooting through my belly urges me to continue. I curl out my finger and beckon him forward.

Mr. Macan stands so close, his body heat warms

my skin. Or perhaps that's the furnace burning deep in my core.

I tilt my head, part my lips, and sweep my gaze to his panting mouth.

"Aileen," he rasps.

"Yes?" I run a finger down his chest.

"What will it take for you to remove that lingerie?"

Chapter Seven

I gaze up at Mr. Macan, my breath shallowing. He's the most dangerous man I know, yet he looks at me like I'm his last supper.

The corner of his mouth lifts into a smile, and my pussy floods with slick heat. Never in my twenty-one years of existence have I felt so attracted, appreciated, or aroused.

Things were different when we hid our identities behind masks. I was free to explore as an anonymous dancer. My mind flickers with all manner of consequences. Losing funding for university, my fiancé's retribution, my family's disappointment and ruin. So much is riding on my marriage to Declan that I can't take any kind of risk.

"Mr. Macan, I can't," I say.

He cocks his head and frowns in a silent command to continue.

"I might be able to explain away the burlesque dancing, but what you're asking for is stripping. If Declan found out—"

"Of course."

He steps back, seeming to blink away his attraction. Even the way he stands changes. He's stiffer and radiates less of the appeal I noticed earlier from the stage. When he angles his body away from mine, my heart sags at the rejection.

"I will speak to my son," he says, sounding formal. "Make him understand he's a lucky little bastard to have such an enchanting fiancée."

Irritation tightens my skin. I clench my teeth, biting back a retort, but the frustration burning through my veins is all-consuming. No amount of words can fix what's wrong with Declan, let alone make him appreciate a woman he doesn't want.

"I've changed my mind," I snap.

"Why?"

"Declan's been cheating on me since the beginning. He even posts his antics on social media." My hands curl into fists. "Maybe it's time I get a little satisfaction."

A line appears between his brows. "You mean retribution?"

"I just want to feel good," I murmur.

"Is that all?" Mr. Macan turns to look me full in the face.

I gulp, my pulse beating harder than the double bass. Why didn't I accept his first proposal to take off my clothes? Because a tiny shard of me wondered if it was a loyalty test—his way of assessing whether or not to end the alliance and throw my family to the sharks. But from the way he's devouring me with those flaming blue eyes, it isn't.

He wants me to be sure about what I'm going to do next. He wants a reason. A reason why I'm willing to dance naked for my fiancé's father, other than revenge.

My tongue darts out to lick my lips, and he drifts closer, as though drawn to the movement.

"When I was up on stage, I could barely take my eyes off you," I murmur. "Then when one of the gentlemen took out his cock, I wished he was you."

His nostrils flare. "Were you naked? Is that why they masturbated?"

Heat rises to my cheeks, spreading down my chin, my collarbones, and chest. I pant through parted lips and murmur, "I was humping the pole."

He stares down at me, his face a blank mask. My stomach twists into a dozen tight knots. Shit. I've said too much, but he would have found out about the pole the moment he spoke to the other gentlemen.

The pulse in my throat beats like the wings of a trapped butterfly. I'm about to blurt an apology when he tightens his jaw and inhales a deep breath.

"Show me," he rasps.

Relief loosens my stomach knots, only to be replaced by a throbbing ache between my legs. I glance around the room, dismissing most of the antique mahogany furniture before my gaze lands on the four-poster. After seeing how badly Jennifer got hurt from a broken pole, the last thing I want to do is molest a bedpost.

Turning back to Mr. Macan, I say, "But I couldn't possibly damage—"

"Use me."

My clit swells, and I have to squeeze my thighs together and stifle a moan. "Grind against your body?"

He nods.

"Mutually assured destruction?" I ask, echoing his words from earlier.

The corner of his mouth lifts into a smile. "Nothing that happens here will leave these walls."

Every inch of my body vibrates in sync with the pounding of my pulse. Fucking hell. This is the point of no return. It's like pausing at the top of a roller coaster and looking down an impossibly steep drop. Worse, because I know without doubt that this is going to be the ride of my life.

"Alright." The word comes out as a low rasp.

I place my hands on his bare chest again, reveling in how his pecs tighten beneath my palms. Peering up at him from beneath my lashes, I steer him toward the cushioned bench.

Mr. Macan is surprisingly compliant for a mobster, letting me push him down to sit. I sway my hips in time to the music, lowering myself into a crouch between his knees, and move his ankles apart to give myself some space.

"Sit on your hands," I say.

"Did your friend teach you this?" he asks, his eyes twinkling.

"Mostly from the content Declan posts online. He has to do this when the girls in his videos give him lap dances."

His lips tighten, and a muscle in his jaw flexes. Good. I want him to know that the precious brat he's trying so hard to reform is a piece of shit. My conscience twangs with a reminder that Mr. Macan is a widower trying to compensate his son for not having a mother, but I remind myself of everything Declan did to make me feel inadequate.

"Why wasn't I informed of this behavior?" He slips his hands beneath his thighs.

"It's not like Declan gave me your direct number."

I offer him a tight smile—my way of showing I'm above Declan's disrespect. What I don't tell him is how much I would endure from his asshole son to secure the family's financial support. Mr. Macan's gaze continues to bore into mine until I run my hands up and down his thighs.

"Being here with you more than makes up for Declan's cheating," I murmur.

Still clutching his legs, I lift my hips, so I'm bending over Mr. Macan with my cleavage in his line of sight. His gaze drops to my breasts, and he pants through parted lips.

Shit. The man wasn't joking when he said I was exactly his type. I've never had anyone look at me with such intensity or need.

The music changes and I straighten, watching his stare travel up my body and fix on my face. With a smile, I turn around, giving him a perfect view of my ass.

Mr. Macan groans, the sound making my folds turn slick. I lower myself onto his crotch and let my weight settle on his muscular thighs. When my pussy grazes his clothed erection, he hisses through his teeth, infusing my skin with delicious shivers.

Then I settle onto his hard length and moan.

There was never any build-up with Declan. He made sure anything we did together was unpleasant, rushed, or humiliating and it was precisely the reason I demanded that we waited until marriage before having sex. He wanted to push me to see how far I could tolerate his mistreatment. It's hard to believe how different things are with mutual attraction.

"Good girl, Mr. Macan growls, breaking me from my thoughts. "You feel so good sitting on my cock."

A thrill of arousal settles between my legs, and I rock back and forth against his length. Pleasure ripples through my core, making me moan. I build up a rhythm, doing all the work of grinding to the music. The heat of his dick stokes the flames of my arousal, making my pussy spasm and clench. He remains still, his hot breath warming the back of my neck.

"You dance exceptionally for a first-timer."

"Th-thank you," I whisper, my voice breathy.

Mr. Macan's deep groan goes straight to my swollen clit. "And you have a beautiful figure."

My cheeks heat, but it's nothing compared to the furnace between my legs. Mr. Macan is the opposite of his son. He's masculine, sophisticated, and appreciative. Everything about this man is incredibly sexy.

Rolling my hips in time to a drum solo, I grind faster against his length, making his breath quicken. His deep groans and heavy panting are equally as arousing as the hard cock providing delicious friction.

I glance over my shoulder, locking gazes. His eyes burn with the kind of fire I've only read about in romance novels. His nostrils flare, and the hard angles of his face tighten, looking like he's about to lose control.

Pressure builds up in my core. I grind and pant, my body chasing the sensation. I'm so wet that I'm sure my juices are soaking through my knickers and into his tuxedo pants.

"Turn around," he rasps, snapping me out of my trance.

I slide off his lap, pivot, and drop into a crouch between his spread thighs. Mr. Macan stares down at me with his pupils dilated. I sweep my gaze down his exposed chest, taking in those prominent pecs and tight abs, and let it settle on the erection straining through his pants.

My fingers twitch toward his fly, and it takes every effort not to unleash his thick cock. There's a part of me that still fears the consequences of getting caught and wants this moment to last.

Holding onto his knees, I rise in a body roll that brushes my breasts against his erection.

"Fuck," he says through his teeth. "Do that again."

I oblige, this time, positioning his clothed cock in the gaps between my cups. His hips rise a fraction off the seat. Just as he slides his hands out from beneath his thighs, I draw back and smirk.

His eyes smolder.

I've never in my life felt so powerful.

He lifts me onto his lap, but I avoid his cock and straddle his thigh with the knee of one leg on the cushioned bench and the foot of the other on the floor. Holding onto his broad shoulders for balance, I ask, "Is that alright?"

Mr. Macan's gaze drops to my lips before rising to meet my eyes. "You did this in front of the other gentlemen?" he asks, his voice urgent.

Nodding, I grind my clit on his leg the way I pleasured myself against that pole. Sparks of pleasure shot through my core, making its muscles quiver. Fuck. This feels incredible. I quicken my pace, wanting more, needing it. If Mr. Macan tossed me on that bed and ordered me to take off my thong, there would be no hesitation.

He holds onto my hips, his breath becoming

more frantic. "And you liked having all those eyes on your body?"

My skin tingles, and I gasp as his fingers dig into my flesh with the perfect mix of pleasure and pain. All I can utter in response is a moaned, "Yes."

"That was very naughty," he says in a deep growl that goes straight to my nipples.

"It was."

He writhes against me, and a moment later, I'm no longer humping his thigh but grinding against a deliciously hard erection. "Did you cum?"

"Not completely," I reply with a gasp.

"What happened?"

I can barely concentrate with his clothed cock so swollen that I feel every ridge. We sit so close together that Mr. Macan's lips graze my ear. My fingers close around his shoulders. I want his teeth to close around my lobe. I want him to pin me down and make me shatter around that juicy, thick length.

"Aileen," he snarls. "I asked you a question. What happened when you tried to cum?"

"Some of the gentlemen rushed the stage. I panicked and escaped."

He draws back, his eyes ablaze. "Did they touch you?"

"The MC held them back while I ran."

"Good girl. As a reward for heading straight to me, you may cum."

I buck my hips, my clit swelling to the point of pain. My pussy is so drenched that I no longer feel the lace of my thong. Every ounce of concentration centers on the pleasure I'm getting from Mr. Macan's thick cock.

Pressure builds up around my core, and the muscles of my pelvis quiver. A tiny voice in the back of my head reminds me that I have an obligation to the family. I can't just ruin everything by grinding on our benefactor's cock. But I'm so hot and wet and close to orgasm that the thought gets drowned out by lust. Mr. Macan grips tighter, moving me so the friction is harder, faster, and unbearably intense.

"When I selected you for my son, I expected you to become a credit to the family," he snarls, his hot breath filling my ear. "Instead, you're flaunting that delectable body in front of other men."

"Yes, sir," I reply, my voice breathy.

"And you pleasure yourself in public."

My teeth clamp down on my bottom lip. I never thought being chastised while on the verge of cumming could be so enjoyable.

"Are you an exhibitionist, Aileen?"

"I-I think so."

"What do you have to say for yourself? He grinds against my clit.

"I'm sorry, sir."

"Sorry for what?"

The most powerful climax explodes through my core, stealing my breath. I convulse around Mr. Macan, my muscles spasming. He holds me tight, his whispered words of reprimand falling on muffled ears.

As the sensations fade, I sag against his chest, spent and shuddering through the aftershocks.

"That doesn't sound at all remorseful." Mr. Macan rubs circles over my back.

"I couldn't help myself," I say between panting breaths.

"You've been a very bad girl," he drawls as I tremble against his larger body. "Very bad indeed. Such behavior cannot go unpunished."

Chapter Eight

I'm still light-headed and jittery from the most intense orgasm of my life when Mr. Macan slides off my wig, pulls off the sheer cap, and unpins my hair.

Mousy brown strands tumble down to my shoulders and brush against my sensitive skin.

"That's better," he says. "I want you to look more like yourself for your punishment."

Punishment.

I gulp.

It's the second time he's said that word.

I have no idea what Mr. Macan is planning, but every fiber in my body tells me that it will be pleasurable.

He twists his fingers through the hair at the base of my skull and pulls back my head with a gentle tug.

My heart skips several beats. Declan has pulled my hair more times than is reasonable, but nobody has ever handled it so sensually.

"You're going to do exactly as I say, Aileen, is that understood?" He tightens his grip on my hair, sending sparks of pleasure across my scalp.

"Yes sir," I whisper.

"Get up." He releases his hold on my hair.

I'm still so unsteady that it doesn't occur to me not to place my hands on his shoulders to steady myself. His huge muscles flex beneath my palms, making my knees buckle. Mr. Macan doesn't reprimand me for touching him, which has to be an encouraging sign.

"Step back," he growls. "Let me take a look at you."

I draw back, my legs still trembling. He makes a circling motion with his index finger, ordering me to turn around.

His sharp intake of breath goes straight to my ego, making me preen under the burn of his gaze.

"Dark hair suits you," is all he says. "Now, take off your heels."

Still mindful of my burlesque training, I bend from the waist, stick out my ass, and make a show of removing my shoes. We both know they come off with a kick, but I want Mr. Macan to enjoy the spectacle.

He exhales a deep, satisfying groan that hits me straight between the legs.

"Good girl," he rasps. "You look so good with that ass in the air, and your knickers soaked with your juices."

I gasp at his words, my thighs involuntarily squeezing shut.

"Keep those legs open."

"Sorry, sir."

Warm fingertips graze one ass cheek, sending a trail of sparks across my skin. I bite down on my lip, wondering if he plans on giving me a spanking, but he pulls back his hand, leaving my heart clenching at the absence of his touch.

"Turn around and take off your corset," he says, his voice a low command.

I straighten in a body roll that makes him groan, perform a shortened version of the three-step turn, and roll my shoulders.

The corners of his lips lift into a smile, and he presses the heel of his hand into his crotch. My gaze drops down to the erection tenting from his tuxedo pants, and I run my tongue along my lips.

Mr. Macan's upper body drifts forward, his gaze bouncing from my eyes to my mouth.

"Do..." I clear my throat, my heart still pounding. "Do you need help with that, sir?"

"Are you offering to suck my cock?" he asks, his voice laced with amusement.

I raise a shoulder. "Just returning the favor."

"If you want to touch this, you'll have to earn the privilege."

Now it's my turn to smile. I see where Declan gets his inflated confidence, only with Mr. Macan, that cockiness is well-deserved.

He sits back, his gaze sweeping down my form. "Do as I say and take off your corset."

This time, I don't hesitate. Swaying my hips to the background music, I unfasten the hooks and let the garment fall to the floor with a gentle thud. His eyes flash, and heat flares between my legs, making my clit swell.

"Good girl," he says, the deep timber of his voice like a caress. "Now, take off your bra."

A pleasant shiver runs down my spine as I follow his order. For someone who resents the lack of control I have over my life, it's exhilarating to undress at the command of a man like Mr. Macan.

The bra drops to the floor, and he beckons me forward. "Take off those pasties and show me your nipples."

I gulp. Both because his order pushes against a

boundary and because following it won't be as easy as peeling off a piece of leather.

"What is it?" he asks.

"Um..." I bite down on my bottom lip. "They're glued on. It's to stop them from falling off when I—"

"Kneel."

My jaw drops. "What?"

Mr. Macan rises to his feet, making me take a step backward. He raises a brow in a silent warning. Everything I know about this man says that now isn't the time to test his limits. The arrangement he made with dad still hangs in the balance.

I drop down to my knees, my gaze zooming in on the obscene bulge in his pants. Oh, shit. He's going to grab me by the back of my hair and fuck my throat. That's what Declan would do before throwing me down and telling me that I'm worthless.

He advances toward me, places his fingers beneath my chin, and tilts up my head so we're locking gazes. The look in his eyes is warm and playful... and confusing.

"Stay there. I'll fetch some body oil to loosen the glue."

"Yes, sir," I whisper, still not understanding why he's being so nice.

He disappears into the bathroom, only to return a moment later with a bottle of oil and a large towel. After resuming his seat, he rolls the towel and places it on the floor beneath his spread legs.

"Come."

I shuffle forward on my knees, but he holds up a hand.

"Crawl."

Oh.

I lower myself onto all fours and crawl over to him in time with the music. His nostrils flare, his gaze dropping down to my swaying breasts.

"Rest your knees on the towel," he says, his voice hoarse.

Stopping between his spread legs, I settle on the folded cotton, my hands resting on his thighs.

He raises his brow at my audacity but doesn't comment, instead unscrewing the cap of the oil and positioning it over my nipple. "I'm going to help you loosen the glue."

"Yes, sir," I murmur.

He drizzles the warm oil over my nipple, coating both the pastie and my skin. Liquid spills down my breast and onto the towel beneath my knees. My breath quickens. This is a first. No one has ever paid me such personal attention, let alone such consideration.

"I'm going to pull it off," he says.

"Please," I whisper.

He slides his finger over the slick patch of skin above my nipple, working the oil beneath the pastie. My skin sizzles at his touch, and my heartbeat kicks up several notches. I shift on my knees, squeeze my thighs together, and hope he doesn't realize I'm so desperately aroused.

"You're tense," he murmurs, his fingers working my nipple.

"I've never worn a pastie before or had anyone remove one."

His deep chuckle fills my chest with a warm glow. It's sensual and rich, reminding me of whiskey and dark chocolate. How could a man like this be Declan's dad?

"That makes two of us," he says.

My gaze snaps up to meet his smiling blue eyes. "Pardon?"

"I've never had to remove a pastie. I hope you're not feeling any discomfort." He peels off a tiny corner of the round piece of leather and works in a little more oil.

I shake my head, my gaze fixed on his fingers.

Bit by bit, he dissolves the glue and eases off the pastie, revealing a hardened nipple.

"That wasn't painful at all," I say with a relieved sigh.

"Good." He rolls my nipple between his thumb and forefinger and leans close, his hot breath fanning against my ear.

In a hoarse whisper, he adds, "Because when I want you to feel pain, it will be intentional."

Chapter Nine

A bolt of arousal shoots straight to my core. I gaze up into Mr. Macan's eyes, which are now glazed over with lust.

Did he just say he was going to hurt me?

I wait for him to elaborate, but he doesn't fill the silence. Instead, his oily fingers close in around my nipple and squeeze.

My pussy clenches. My clit pulses in response. I bite down on my bottom lip to suppress a moan. Ah. That's what he means by intentional pain.

"Eyes on me," he says, his voice harsh.

I drag my gaze up to meet pupils so dilated that his irises are a tiny ring of blue. Without any further explanation, he releases my nipple and moves his attention to my other breast.

Each drizzle of oil, each slide of his fingers, makes

my clit thrum with need. I need those fingers working my pussy until I come apart under his touch.

My head spins. My breath comes in shallow pants. I'm in over my head. He's barely touched my nipples yet I'm drifting toward the bulge in his tuxedo pants. The fabric stretches over his erection, highlighting every ridge and vein. I want to pull down his zipper and unleash that huge cock.

What is wrong with me? I should be afraid, not aroused. I should be focused on the family's future, not frantic to fuck.

I barely notice the removal of the second pastie until his fingers close in around that nipple.

"You have such gorgeous breasts," he says, his gaze locked on my face. He pinches both nipples, sending twin bolts of sensation to my core.

My back arches, and I release a moan. A heavy drumbeat pounds between my ears in sync with the one behind my clit. At this point, I'm beyond blushing. The heat burning my cheeks has traveled down my neck and spread across my chest.

"Th-thank you," I croak.

He leans in close enough so my nostrils fill with the scent of his aftershave, a heady blend of cedarwood and musk that derails my train of thought. His lips are so close to my ear that I can feel his heat.

"Let's continue your punishment," he says, his voice a deep rumble. "Stand up and take off your thong."

His fingers release my nipples, leaving them throbbing for his touch. He draws back, removing his warmth and scent.

"Now."

At his command, I scramble to my feet, my gaze still fixed on his face. My senses are so attuned to his touch that its absence makes me feel vulnerable and deprived. My heart pounds so hard, I feel its vibrations in the tips of my fingers, which tremble as I reach for the waistband of my thong.

He raises a finger, making me pause. "Slowly."

The music drifts back to my awareness, reminding me that this is still a dance. Rolling my shoulders and hips, I turn around so he has a full view of my ass.

Mr. Macan's deep groan fills my spirit with a fresh burst of confidence. I glance over my shoulder, gaze at him through my lashes and ease the thong down my hips.

His lips part, and he breathes hard, his gaze bouncing from my ass to my thighs. The sight of him looking so horny makes fluid stream down my thigh.

"Are you wet for me, Aileen?" he asks.

"Yes, sir."

"Show me."

I slide the thong down my legs and step out and away from the fabric.

"Give that to me," he rasps.

My gaze drops to the discarded underwear. In a graceful forward bend, I pick it up and hold it out to him.

He takes it, his fingers brushing mine, sending pleasant tingles up my hand. I straighten, my chest heaving as he brings it to his nose, takes a deep sniff, and groans.

"You smell sweeter than I expected."

Excitement kicks me in the heart. When did he start thinking of me like that? Tonight, when I was Miss Demeanor and he was Mr. Burgundy, or earlier?

I hold my tongue, not wanting to ruin the moment, and don't even comment when he slides my thong into the pocket of his tuxedo pants.

Mr. Macan sits back in his seat, his gaze dragging down my naked form. My nipples tighten under his stare, and I squeeze my thighs together.

"Let's list your transgressions." He counts them off on his manicured fingers. "Clandestine burlesque dancing, public masturbation, and entering a strange man's room for a private dance—"

"But you're not a stranger," I blurt.

DANCE FOR DADDY

"I'm your future father-in-law?" he asks, his features stern. "Is that what you mean to say?"

My shoulders sag at the reminder of Declan, but I still manage to nod. Everything he's said so far makes me seem like a terrible fiancée—someone about to jeopardize the much-needed alliance to save my family.

"Is the deal off, now?" I whisper.

"That's entirely up to you," he replies. "What do you want?"

I lick my lips, my mind whirring. If I had a fairy godmother, I would wish Declan didn't make me late to meet Jennifer, so she wouldn't have broken her leg.

But that's thinking too small.

What I really want is for Mr. Macan to give me a night of pleasure and go ahead with the deal. What I truly want is for him to break the engagement that neither I nor my fiancé want.

But that might be asking too much.

He raises his brows, indicating that I should answer.

"Please don't punish my family for my mistakes," I say, my words guarded. "They don't know what I did. And they can't. Please, punish me instead."

Surprise flickers across his features, although I'm not sure why. As much as I enjoyed all that male attention, I don't want Declan to twist this situation into something it's not. He's the type of thug who would make me dance for his druggie friends, while they and his hired blondes serenade me with mocking laughter.

"Come here." He taps his lap.

"Sir?" I whisper.

"You asked to be punished, yes?" He cocks his head. "Lie on my lap. I'm going to spank that sweet ass of yours until you learn you either cry or cum."

A bolt of arousal shoots straight to my clit. I step backward, but Mr. Macan drags me onto his lap, pushes my head down, and secures me with a forearm across my back.

His huge erection stabs into my side, and I swear I can feel its bulbous cockhead.

"Now, Aileen," he snarls in my ear, "it's time you made up for your transgressions."

"Yes, sir," I whisper.

His large hands stroke the curve of my hips, sending pleasant shivers down my spine. I arch my back and part my thighs in response, desperate for his touch.

"Now, list them." A large, warm hand strokes my ass cheek, and I sigh into his touch.

"Um... Dancing in public."

He raises his hand and delivers a hard slap.

DANCE FOR DADDY

Stinging pain spreads across my ass cheek, making me open my mouth in a silent scream. I take another breath, but before I can cry out, Mr. Macan slips his hand between my legs, parts my wet folds, and rubs the pad of his thumb on my swollen clit.

Pleasure races low in my belly, and I roll my hips against his hands, trying to deepen the friction. He quickens his strokes, bringing me close to the edge.

Electricity shoots through my veins, and my skin breaks out in a sweat. I'm gasping at the exquisite mixture of pleasure and pain, my eyes rolling toward the back of my head.

Pressure builds up around my core, and the muscles tense. I'm so close—ready to cum. "Please," I whisper. "Don't stop."

He pulls back his hand, leaving me crying out for more.

Instead of finishing the job and making me climax, he says, "And the second transgression?"

"Public masturbation."

"With a stripper pole, no less."

I groan, my body going limp. Hearing it the second time only makes it worse.

Another slap lands on my ass cheek, this one hard enough to send sensation straight to my needy clit. I squeeze my eyes shut and choke out a sob.

At this rate, I'm more likely to cry before I cum.

Mr. Macan's thick fingers find my clit once more, this time with circular strokes that give me a whirlpool of ecstasy. My legs tremble, and the muscles of my pussy clench and release. The wet sounds I'm making are so obscene, I'm glad he can't see my face.

I rock back and forth, my clit swelling. Biting my lip, I hold back my words. I'm so close to cumming.

"The next transgression?" He pulls away his hand.

My arms and legs sag. "Um... I went to a strange man's room for a private dance, even though that's you."

His next slap makes my back arch. "Just for that, I'm adding an extra spank for your cheek."

"Aaah!" My toes curl.

He parts my thighs further, exposing more of my bare pussy. As he caresses my clit, the pad of this thumb brushes against my opening.

Oh, fuck.

I need those fingers.

Right now.

"What do you have to say for yourself?" he growls, his fingers stroking up and down my swollen clit.

"S-sorry." I buck my hips, trying to get him to fill

me with something, anything, especially the hot, thick erection pressing into my side.

He rubs faster, filling my ears with that filthy, wet sound of my own juices. "Naughty girl. I think you enjoyed making a spectacle of yourself in public."

I did. Even more so, now that I'm facing the immediate consequences. My lips part to release a moan, and he withdraws his hand.

Tears gather in the corners of my eyes. I'm aching. Aching for release. No one has ever gotten me to the brink of orgasm so many times. No one has ever gotten me even close. This is the most exquisite form of torture.

"And the final transgression?" he asks.

Shivering, I bite down on my bottom lip and raise my hips, eager for the next spank.

"Backtalk," I say with a moan.

He slaps my ass cheek so hard that my entire lower body vibrates, and I choke out a sob. Tears of pain, frustration, and anticipation gather in the corners of my eyes. If he leaves me unfulfilled it will be the worst form of punishment.

His digits slide through my wet folds again and pause at my entrance. "Will you be a good girl for me and cum around my fingers or will I have to put you in the corner?"

The words tumble from my lips in a moan. "I'll be good."

His middle and index fingers breach my opening, entering me with a delicious stretch. "So tight," he rasps. "Am I your first?"

"Um..." I shake my head, pushing away the few awkward and humiliating experiences with Declan. "Not exactly."

Dildos count, don't they? According to Declan, they do. As do blowjobs and fingering. To my relief, Mr. Macan doesn't ask me to elaborate and correctly assumes that I did a few things with his son.

Ugh.

I don't want to think of that asshole. Not when I'm having the most exciting experience of my life. I tilt my hips, giving him better access, and he slides his fingers down to the knuckle.

My walls adjust to the intrusion, clenching and closing around the thick digits until the pad of his thumb ghosts gentle circles over the fine hairs of my asshole. Sparks of pleasure skitter across my skin, and I tighten around his fingers.

He pumps his digits in and out of me while his thumb presses down my pucker. I can't tell which sensation is more electrifying—the threat that he might breach my asshole, or the pleasure simmering in my core.

I buck my hips, arch my back, and ride his fingers. The digit not inside my pussy brushes rough strokes over my clit, making it pulse in time with his movements. Pressure mounts like water boiling in a teakettle. I'm so close.

"Naughty girl." His fingers stop, and he grabs a handful of my hair. "You are not allowed to take control."

"S-sorry, sir," I groan.

My entire body is a raw nerve, desperate for the next touch to send me over the precipice.

"Do you still want me to make you cum?" he asks.

"Yes… Please," I say from between clenched teeth.

He moves his fingers at a much slower pace, keeping me simmering over the edge, but it's not enough for me to cum.

"Beg me, Aileen." His voice is so deep and rich that it coats my skin with warm velvet. "Tell me how much you want that orgasm."

"Please, sir. Make me cum."

The fingers continue their maddeningly languid caresses, barely grazing my clit. Goosebumps pimple across my arms and legs, and it feels like every hair on my body is standing on end.

"Go on," he says, his voice coaxing.

"If you let me cum, I'll—"

"You'll what?"

"I'll give you anything," I blurt.

His rich chuckle warms my skin. "Good girl. Since you asked so prettily, I will give you what you need."

He flicks my clit, and I boil over with hot cascades of pleasure. The release is so intense that my mind blanks, and my vision goes white. My pussy spasms around his fingers, infusing the rest of my body with liquid euphoria. I convulse on his lap, my arm brushing against his impossibly thick cock.

Blood roars between my ears, and my pulse beats so loudly that I can barely make out Mr. Macan's whispered words of encouragement. He rubs my back as I gasp and pant through the orgasm until it fades to gentle aftershocks.

As my body slumps, he pulls me upright and seats me on his lap. My muscles still tingle, leaving me feeling so boneless I rest my head against his neck.

"That's it, beautiful," he says, his voice soothing. "Let it all out."

I'm still panting, still trembling, still reveling in the glow of my release that I'm not sure I correctly hear what he says next.

"You did so well," he rumbles. "Now, let's see how you perform in front of an audience."

Chapter Ten

Mr. Macan continues cradling me in my arms as I come down from the high of my second orgasm. My head rests on his broad shoulders, with my ass cheeks pressing into his cock.

It's so hot and hard and hefty that I can't help imagining what it would feel like to split me open. Would he be gentle or rough? Would he hold onto my hair and take me from behind, or would we have sex face to face?

His large hand makes soothing circles on my back, and he's still whispering words of praise when it finally registers.

"Sir?" I ask.

"Hmmm?"

"What did you mean about performing in front of an audience?"

The hand rubbing my back doesn't falter. "You seem to be an exhibitionist. Having men watch you turns you on?"

I lick my lips. "Yes, but I don't want them rushing on the stage like last time."

"That won't happen. Firstly, there will be no stage. Secondly, you'll have a choice."

"What kind?" I draw back and meet his gaze.

His eyes are half-lidded, still filled with lust, and the set of his face is relaxed. I can't believe this is Declan's dad, a man known for tearing through an entire rival gang, a man everyone knows not to cross.

"You can choose to perform behind a pane of glass that separates you from your audience or in the confines of a four-poster with three or four of my friends looking in from the outside."

Heat floods my pussy, and my nipples tighten. "Do you trust these men not to get on the bed?"

"Nobody touches you if they want to keep their hands."

"And you trust them?"

His laughter is warm and rich, making me relax against his broad chest. It's strange that barely two hours have passed and I feel like I already trust him.

"Yes, Aileen," he says. "We all play within set boundaries we know not to cross."

My mind conjures up an image of Mr. Macan cavorting with a leggy blonde while three men stroke their cocks on the perimeter of a four-poster bed. She looks exactly like the models Declan hires for social media.

"So, you've done this before?" I blurt.

His hand slides up my spine, up the nape of my neck, and cradles the back of my head. All traces of amusement vanish, and he looks me straight in the eyes.

"Sometimes, I watch from the sidelines, but this will be my first time on the bed."

"Why?" The word slips from my lips before I can stop myself.

"I haven't found anyone I wanted enough," he murmurs.

My throat thickens, and my heart sinks a little from its resting place. Everyone knows that he's been alone since someone from the Fian gang murdered his wife, but it sounds like he might have been celibate.

"What about in private—"

"No." He rubs the pad of his thumb over my cheekbone. "You'll be my first woman in over two decades."

The ache in my chest deepens, and my stomach tightens at the prospect of being the first woman since his wife. Mr. Macan is handsome, rich, powerful, and well-dressed. He's part of a much larger organization that's rumored to value marriage.

Lots of women would kill for a chance to be with this man, yet he's overlooking them for the girl who he caught dancing burlesque behind the family's back.

I can't help myself, but I have to ask, "Why do you want me?"

He draws so close that the heat of his body makes mine break into a sweat. "Don't you think I would choose the best woman available for my son?"

My brows draw together. "Yes, but wasn't that a business arrangement?"

"I'm not in the habit of investing in construction firms, Aileen," he says. "When Gerald came to me for help, I was going to turn him down until I remembered he had a promising daughter."

"And that's why you set up the alliance?" I ask. "Because you liked me?"

"I thought you would be the perfect companion for my youngest." His eyes sparkle. "You're beautiful, curvaceous, hard-working, intelligent, and compassionate."

My gaze drops down to his chest. We've known

the Macan family for years, but I never thought a man like Mr. Macan would notice me. He has to be talking about one of my sisters. They're all outgoing and keep up with the latest in hair and makeup and fashion, while I'm the one known to take comfort in books.

Even Declan admits that the Walsh sisters are all beauties, except for me. He thinks all the barbs and bullying will pressure me into becoming more like them, but I've always hated being the center of attention.

Until now.

"So you think I have the potential to be more like my sisters?" I ask.

He shakes his head. "My other sons used to point you and your sisters out at events. You were the one whose nose was always in a book and never on her phone. I asked around to see what kind of girl you were and what I heard was impressive."

"Oh," I whisper. "What did they say?"

"You're one of the few young women connected to our world who doesn't seem to obsess over money and status symbols. You've kept the same small group of friends even though none of them are rich. And you spend more time at home than in night-clubs," he says. "Loyalty, integrity and family values go a long way in this world."

"But to answer the question about your sisters, I thought you were perfect the way you are. I thought Declan would benefit from a modest young woman who could keep his feet on the ground. Someone who would challenge him to be a better man."

A bitter laugh explodes from my chest. "He likes tall blondes he can flaunt on social media."

He cups my cheeks with both hands, holding me in place so we're looking eye to eye. His gaze burns with an intensity I can barely withstand.

"Aileen, I want to ask you once more. Are you happy with my son?"

The air thickens with so much tension that it's hard to even breathe, let alone hold his gaze. I lower my lashes, trying to think of a way to answer that question that won't lead to him abandoning my family.

"Aileen," he says, his voice gentle. "Does Declan make you happy?"

"No," I whisper.

"Explain."

"He's vicious, cruel, disrespectful."

"How?" he asks.

I swallow hard. "Declan's always flaunting other women and complaining that I'm not like them. He hates that I'm at university while he dropped out.

He's always dragging me to places where people do drugs. And..."

My breath hitches.

Gosh, I feel so exposed, spilling out my guts while I'm still naked. For reasons I still don't understand, Mr. Macan thinks I'm beautiful. What if telling him more about how Declan treats me changes his mind?

"Tell me," he says, his voice firm.

"He calls me ugly, fat, four-eyes."

"He's a bloody idiot," Mr. Macan growls. "Look at me."

My gaze sweeps up to his face. All traces of amusement have vanished, leaving his features angular and harsh. White flecks stand out within his blue irises, making them look like they're on fire.

"You know that nothing Declan's told you is true," he says.

I glance down at his collarbones, trying to think of how to respond without sounding weak. "It's not like I've ever been showered with compliments. Hearing those insults every day can wear down a person's confidence."

Everything I've said so far is an understatement. Declan didn't just disparage my appearance, he invited others to do the same. It's hard to keep one's composure when all of Declan's drug friends are so willing to throw me under the bus to get cozy with the rich boy.

"Aileen?" he asks. "After tonight, you have to know how much men appreciate your beauty."

My shoulders rise to my ears. "I was just playing a role."

"While exposing your delectable little body," he says, his voice warm. "It wasn't the wig or the mask or the dance moves that made us all salivate. It was you."

Pleasant tingles race across my skin, making me smile. I hate being the type of person who needs external validation, but a year of being engaged to Declan has eroded my self-esteem to rubble.

"Now, will you answer another question?" he asks.

"What is it?" I whisper.

"Do you want to be engaged to my son?"

I bite down on my bottom lip. If I had a choice, I wouldn't be in the same room as Declan, let alone engaged to the little bastard.

The hands cupping my cheeks spread down my neck and hold my shoulders. The grip is firm but not painful. His hands radiate warmth and much-needed reassurance.

I'm already in trouble. I've already been caught

doing something I shouldn't. I may as well tell the truth.

"What about the alliance?" I ask.

"I want to know about you," he says.

"What would you do if I said no?" I whisper. "Would you pull back your support?"

"Aileen," he growls.

My stomach lurches, but I'm more afraid of loan sharks coming after the family than I am of Mr. Macan. He's the type of man who would kill you and be done, but the rumors I've heard about sharks are enough to give a person nightmares. Debt collectors don't just sell your possessions, they sell your daughters. And if they don't raise enough to pay off what you owe, then they sell your organs.

Marriage to Declan is the best of two terrible outcomes.

"I don't like him, but I don't have a choice," I mutter.

He doesn't speak for several heartbeats, but his grip tightens. His hot breath fans the side of my face, making my insides twist.

This is the moment he'll switch from kindness to cruelty. The moment he'll tell me that I don't have a choice and must turn his worthless brat into a useful member of society. The moment he'll give me a terrible ultimatum.

My heart beats hard and fast, as though it's trying to escape my chest and skitter under the bed. I don't blame it. Especially not after I just suggested I'm being coerced.

Tension presses down on me from all sides, pushing down on my back, my throat, and my lungs. Black spots appear on the edges of my vision, and I force air into my lungs, determined not to faint.

After what feels like an eternity, he loosens his grip on my shoulders.

"Would you consider being mine?" he asks.

Chapter Eleven

Mr. Macan's question is like a punch to the heart, making me bolt upright.

Would I consider a handsome older man who gives me orgasms? Would I consider a man I find irresistible? Would I consider a man who wants me as much as I want him?

"Wait." Words tumble from my lips. "You'd have me?"

"I realize my mistake when choosing you for my son," he replies. "Instead of asking him for the type of fiancée he wanted, I chose the girl I thought would be perfect for me."

His gaze sweeps down my nude body and settles on my lips, making me flush.

"You always seemed like such a nice young

woman, but uncovering this side of your personality has made you irresistible."

Heat gathers between my thighs. I shift on his lap, trying to ignore my arousal. An impossible feat, since I'm also sitting on that thick cock.

Shit. This man now knows my every secret, has seen me laid bare, and he's prepared to take me for himself.

"Is it my reputation?" he asks. "I know the rumors about my past—"

"No," I say. "It's not that."

"Then what?"

"You'd really take me away from Declan?"

"Yes," he growls. "Whatever you decide, the alliance will still stand."

My eyes squeeze shut. He means what he's saying. Every word. But there's a part of me that can't believe I could be so lucky.

Mr. Macan's reputation doesn't just extend to killing the people involved in the death of his wife. He's known as the perpetual widower. Known as the man who loved his wife so dearly that he never wanted any other woman.

The only time Declan was ever half-decent to me was when there was no one around to give him a handjob or suck his cock. He'd be full of apologies for his shitty behavior followed by promises to be better. Then everything would change once I made him cum.

His tactics no longer work on me, but what if he learned how to manipulate from his father? What if they're both the same kind of man and Mr. Macan rejects me the moment he climaxes?

A tense silence fills the air, broken only by the pounding of my heart. I want this man so much that it hurts. But is one evening of pleasure worth the consequences?

He threads his fingers through my hair, sending tingles down my neck.

"Don't decide now," he murmurs. "If you need to leave—"

"No," I blurt, my gaze snapping to his face. "I mean yes."

His brows rise. "Yes to..."

"Yes to breaking off my engagement with Declan," I reply with a firm nod. "Yes to the four-poster bed, yes to being yours. Yes to—"

His lips descend on mine with a kiss so hungry and urgent that I melt against his chest with a moan. I wrap my arms around his neck, my fingers threading through his silky hair. Hair that's clean and loose and not matted with cornrows and gel.

Firm lips tease mine until my vision fills with

stars. His breath is minty and fresh with a hint of whiskey. I lose myself in the kiss and moan.

Everything about Mr. Macan is different from Declan—his muscular frame, his masculine scent, and the meaty cock lying flush against my pussy.

His tongue slides between my lips and twists with mine.

I could kiss this man for hours and it wouldn't be enough. I could kiss him until I can't breathe and never want for air. I need him deep inside me, filling the void in my heart that Declan could never touch.

When he kisses me like this, all thoughts of alliances and fiancés and exhibitionism drift into the ceiling, leaving me with a man I desire with every fiber of my being.

"Fuck, Aileen," he growls into the kiss. "You make me lose control."

"Likewise," I whisper.

He pulls back, his eyes glazed. "I want the others to see what they can't have. I want them to know I've got the most desirable woman who's ever performed at the club."

His words trigger another bolt of arousal. This is going to be even more exciting than humping a stripper pole.

DANCE FOR DADDY

Mr. Macan texts three of his friends to watch us on the four-poster. As soon as they confirm they can join us, we get dressed. I'm wearing a mask that covers the top half of my face, my blonde wig, the leather skirt, and the matching top. And of course, the heels.

Mr. Macan's upper half is covered by a burgundy smoking jacket that was provided by the room, but he still wears his tuxedo pants.

Our fingers spark as he takes my hand and walks us through the club's wide hallway and down to a set of double doors. They lead to the viewing room, which is named as such because it overlooks the stage, while there's a four-poster in the middle with seating for gentlemen to observe their friends fucking the dancers.

My heart beats in double time to our steps. I can't tell if this is a dream or an erotic nightmare where I'll wake up to Mr. Macan coming to his senses and dumping me on my ass.

Its interior is just as he described. It's located about a story above the stage with its entire left wall overlooking a pair of identically dressed women tap-dancing to an audience of seated gentlemen. The Master of Ceremonies stands at the edge of the stage, holding a pair of sequined hats.

The bed is to the left of the room but not against

the wall. I suppose that's for whoever wants to watch the action from behind the headboard. There are even a few armchairs positioned a few feet away from the bed in case the voyeurs want to watch from a distance.

Sweat breaks out across my brow. I swallow back the heart fluttering in the back of my throat, but nothing can calm my stomach. The flock of butterflies living there is rioting.

It's really happening. I'm about to give the performance of my life. In a moment, his friends will enter the room and stroke their cocks while watching me get fucked. I feel out of my depth.

Mr. Macan squeezes my hand. "Are you alright?"

My gaze snaps back to meet his darkened eyes, his features alight with desire.

"Of course," I say. "I'm excited to be here."

"You're trembling."

He releases my hand and cradles my face. "Say the word if you want to go back to the room. Or if you're having second thoughts about me—"

"No," I blurt. "I want to do this."

"You're sure?"

I give him a shaky nod. "It's just stage fright. That's all."

His eyes soften. "Pick a safe word."

"What?"

DANCE FOR DADDY

"I need a word to let me know at any point if you want this to stop. If you want the spectators to leave or if anything or anyone makes you uncomfortable."

Prickly heat flares across my cheeks. This feels like something out of Fifty Shades, but it's not a bad idea. "How about red?"

He nods. "That will stop the scene. Which word do you choose to slow the scene?"

"Amber, like with the traffic lights?"

"And green is more?" he asks with a grin.

I nod, my chest tightening. The butterflies in my stomach settle, and the fluttering travels between my legs. It's comforting to know that he's giving me control over the scene. I no longer feel so overwhelmed.

A knock sounds on the door.

Mr. Macan's hands drift down to my shoulders, his eyes crinkling with a smile. "One last chance to back out."

"You've been teasing me with your cock all evening, and now's my chance to have a taste." I rock forward on the balls of my feet and place a kiss on his lips.

His eyes widen and his features fall blank. My stomach twists. Did I just overstep some unwritten boundary? It was just a kiss. Why's he looking so shocked? His nostrils flare, and his blue irises ignite with flames of lust. He wraps an arm around my waist and pulls me into his chest.

"Such naughty language," he growls. "Don't worry, Miss Demeanor, I will give you as much cock as your pretty mouth and pussy can handle."

A giggle bubbles up in my chest, making the butterflies scatter. "Let's do this."

He turns to the door. "Enter."

Mr. White Tuxedo walks in, his steps faltering, his gaze raking up and down my form. Without taking his eyes off me, he grins. "So, you're the lucky bastard who got the first private dance."

I press my lips together to suppress a smile.

Two other gentlemen walk in behind Mr. White, revealing the fourth, who's too preoccupied with what's on the screen of his smartphone to notice his surroundings.

Although I can't see his face, I recognize him from the strawberry blond cornrows pulled back to form a ponytail.

It's Declan.

Chapter Twelve

Shock hits me in the gut, shoving all the air out of my lungs. What's left is a roiling sense of revulsion that makes me gag. What kind of twit wants to watch their dad fuck? Mr. Macan releases my waist, strides to the door, and shoves Declan back into the hallway.

I pivot, my face jerking away from the door, and hide my features with the blonde wig.

"Hello." Mr. White offers me his hand. "Sean Riordan. It's a pleasure to meet you."

"Likewise." My voice falters as he brings my knuckles to his lips and continues with a stream of compliments about my dance.

The other two gentlemen keep a respectful distance, seeming more interested in the father-son discussion taking place at the doorway.

"What are you doing here?" Mr. Macan hisses.

"I was in the middle of making a video when I saw Liam." He nods toward the shorter of the gentlemen. "I heard you've got a girl in the observation room, and I wanted to check her out."

"Leave."

Declan rises on his tiptoes. "She's fucking sexy. Will you give me her number?"

My jaw tightens. I thought he only liked skinny blondes. Maybe he only likes women he can control.

"Out," Mr. Macan growls.

"Alright, alright, keep your hair on, Dad," Declan says, his voice cowed. "I only wanted to say hello. You never get any women. All this time, I thought you were gay."

The air fills with a tense silence, broken only by Mr. White's attempts to book me for a private dance at his apartment. I'm too anxious about the tense standoff at the doorway to muster up a coherent excuse.

Mr. White waves his business card under my nose. "If you change your mind—"

"As I said, coming here to perform was a one-off," I mutter.

"A pity." He slips the card back into his pocket. "Don't hesitate if you ever get bored."

I give him a tight smile.

DANCE FOR DADDY

Any other time, I would preen to be in the position to reject a handsome man who's wealthy enough to be a member of this gentlemen's club, but my nerves are frazzled from almost getting caught by my fiancé.

Fuck Declan.

Can't he even let me enjoy this ego boost?

Mr. Macan steps forward, his body pushing Declan further out into the hallway. The door swings shut behind them, leaving me alone in a room with three eager-looking gentlemen.

Some of the anxiety from earlier dissipates, and I can finally breathe. There's no way Declan will get past his father. I turn my attention away from the door and back to the men. The desire in their gazes makes the pulse between my legs pound. Mr. White takes a respectful step backward as though already acknowledging that I belong to Mr. Macan.

Heat gathers in my pussy, and moisture slicks my folds. It's almost as though there's a pane of glass separating me from the men that none of them can cross in Mr. Macan's absence.

The air thrums with anticipation, making my skin tingle. Before I can even bask in the feeling of being desired, the door swings open again.

Mr. Macan steps in, his face set in a hard mask. My heart plummets. He didn't look this furious when earlier in the evening he thought I was some kind of mole sent by his enemies. Shit. Shit. Shit. He's probably angry with himself for everything we did together.

I lower my gaze to the floor, my stomach tightening with dread. Is this the moment he comes to his senses and changes his mind about fucking his son's fiancée in front of three other men?

When he turns the lock, my shoulders sag with relief. I exhale a long breath, my heart stuttering.

It's about to go down.

The other men part as Mr. Macan strides toward me and takes my hand. Without another word, he walks us to a table I didn't notice before and turns around a chair.

"You remember your safe words?" he says.

"Yes, sir," I whisper.

"How are you feeling right now?"

I swallow, my gaze darting around at the men positioning themselves at respectful distances around where we stand. "Green."

Still holding my hand, he sits on the chair, turns to the shorter of the men, and says, "Liam, get Miss Demeanor a large cushion."

Liam flinches at Mr. Macan's tone, which implies he should count himself lucky not to be punished for telling Declan. Liam rushes to the bed,

DANCE FOR DADDY

grabs a huge velvet pillow and plac[...]
Macan's spread legs.

"Angus, I'm sorry," Liam mur[...]
idea your son would—"

"Don't sour the mood," Mr. Macan growls.

With another whispered apology, Liam bobs his head and steps back. I'm surprised he didn't kick the other man out, but maybe that's because Declan might still be lurking on the other side of the door.

Eyes softening, he turns to meet my gaze. "Kneel."

I drop to my knees, my vision zoomed in on the erection thickening in his pants. The cushion beneath my shins is soft yet firm, and its velvet pile brushes against my already sensitized skin. My breath quickens, and my clit pulses between my already slick folds.

Glancing up, I meet his hooded eyes. He breathes fast through parted lips and watches me with such naked desire that my pussy tightens at the intensity of his stare.

Someone on my left groans. Mr. White's arm moves in my periphery, and he pushes the heel of his hand into his crotch.

Fuck, this is already hotter than being onstage.

"What do you want, Miss Demeanor?" Mr. Macan asks.

our cock," I whisper.

"Say it louder for the other gentlemen," he replies, his voice chiding.

My tongue darts out to lick my lips. This is all part of the performance. "I want your cock, sir. Please, let me suck it."

Mr. White groans, and Liam clears his throat. The fact that I'm affecting them with just my words gives me the most pleasant rush.

"Take it out," Mr. Macan says.

My palms are already slick with sweat, but it's nothing compared to what's going on between my legs. With trembling fingers, I fumble at the buttons on the fly of his tuxedo pants to find he's not wearing boxers.

The crown of cock springs out, and I jerk backward. It's flushed a deep shade of red, even more bulbous than I imagined, and leaking with a bead of precum. My lips part and I drift forward, my tongue rubbing at the roof of my mouth.

I reach into his pants and ease out the longest, thickest, veiniest shaft. Declan must have gotten his cock from his mother's side of the family because he isn't even half as blessed as his father. I swallow back a moan but can't contain the sound.

"Fuck," someone growls.

I'm too mesmerized at his impossible length and

girth to appreciate that one of the gentlemen is aroused.

Mr. Macan raises a brow. "Problems?"

"It's just so…" I clear my throat. "Huge."

Someone behind me chuckles. I think it's Mr. White.

"Take your time," Mr. Macan says, his eyes warm.

It's all the encouragement I need to move forward and run the flat of my tongue over his leaking slit.

He grabs my shoulder and hisses through his teeth. "Good girl," he rumbles. "Show my friends how well you can take my cock."

I grab hold of the base of his shaft, my fingers barely touching, and steady my weight on his cloth-covered thigh. Oh, fuck. I'm not sure if it will fit in my mouth, but I'll try.

Out of the corner of my eye, I see Liam already stroking himself through his pants. Movement from the other side also suggests the others are doing the same.

Holding him steady, I swirl my tongue around the huge crown, coating it with a trail of saliva. He shivers, and my chest swells with a thrill of satisfaction. Declan always made a show of telling me I couldn't do anything right.

I push away thoughts of my soon-to-be ex and run my hand up and down Mr. Macan's shaft. Veins bulge beneath my palm as though my touch is making him swell. I close my lips around the ridge of his glans and give it a gentle suck.

"Just like that," he moans. "You're doing so well."

The atmosphere grows heavy with the gentlemen's rapid breaths and my skin tingles with the weight of their stares. I can't believe they're enjoying this as much as I am.

Encouraged by their responses, I part my lips and take Mr. Macan into my mouth. My jaw opens wider as I inch down, taking in as much of him as will fit. Inhaling his masculine scent, I let his smooth cockhead glide over my tongue and fill my mouth with his salty tang.

His breath stills for a second, as though he can't believe I'm really sucking his cock, before restarting with rapid and shallow pants. His abdominal muscles tighten with each sharp exhale, making me wonder when he loosened the smoking jacket.

My arousal mounts with each stroke of my tongue, and my clit pulses with need. I'm naked beneath my leather top and skirt, but even that feels so restrictive. I just want to take it all off.

There's a part of me that wants him to grab my

DANCE FOR DADDY

hair and guide my head, to buck his hips and drive further down my throat. From the way his fingers caress the side of my neck, I can tell he's focused on putting me at ease.

Loosening my jaw, I bob up and down, taking him as far as I can down to the back of my mouth. His large hand settles on the back of my head, and he pushes down with enough pressure to guide my movements.

"You look so pretty with my cock down your throat," he says, his voice hoarse.

I moan around my mouthful, making his fingers tighten around my head. Heat rushes straight to my pussy. I clench hard, and warm liquid trickles down my thigh.

Swallowing around him, I create a little suction that makes him throw his head back. "Fuck, Miss Demeanor, you're so good at this."

"She is," someone adds with a groan.

Pride flares in my chest. I would preen but my mouth is too full.

The gentlemen continue to watch me pumping and sucking that delicious, huge cock, all the while complimenting how well I'm handling his girth. From the movement from all sides, it looks like they're enjoying the show.

It's so easy to get lost in a blowjob, to let my eyes

flutter shut and focus on the salty tang of his precum and hard length sliding over my tongue.

My motions grow more frantic, and Mr. Macan's abs tighten. With a gentle grip on my shoulder, he pulls me off his cock.

"Well done," he says through panting breaths.

My stomach plummets, and I shove back the irrational feeling of being rejected. Even Declan never made me stop halfway through a blow job.

"But I wasn't finished," I say.

Mr. White moans. "What an eager girl."

Standing, Mr. Macan helps me to my feet and gazes down at me, his eyes brimming with warmth. "We're moving to the bed. Let's show my friends how well your wet pussy fits around my cock."

Chapter Thirteen

The gentlemen draw backward as Mr. Macan walks me to the four-poster. From the practiced ease of their movements, I can tell that they've watched each other fuck women multiple times.

They're like a small pack of wolves in tuxedos, their gazes traveling over my body. I wonder if they've ever done more than just watch. My pulse quickens at that thought, and my skin breaks out in a sweat. The only reason I'm so comfortable with the situation is because Mr. Macan is in charge, and he's the only one allowed to touch.

"Take off your clothes," he says. "Let them see the delectable body they can't have."

Someone groans. I'm too focused on Mr. Macan's glistening cock to consider any of the other gentlemen. Somewhere between the moment Declan tried to enter the room and now, he's already removed his shirt. His tuxedo pants are already off, revealing muscular thighs.

Pussy clenching at the sight of his glistening cock, I unfasten my top in time to the music seeping in from the stage. Cool air swirls around my damp skin, tightening my nipples.

"Fuck," one of the men growls. "Who would have thought you were hiding those underneath the pasties?"

A smile curves my lips, and I slide off my skirt, making sure to give my hips a tantalizing wiggle.

The air fills with appreciative moans and gasps, and I feel like a fucking goddess.

"Turn around," Mr. Macan rasps.

With delicate little side steps, I turn in a circle, only for Mr. Macan to join me at the foot of the bed and press his cock against my spine.

"So beautiful." He caresses my ass with his palm while cupping my breast with his other hand.

"Delicious," says Mr. White from behind.

Pride makes my chest swell. I glance from side to side, reveling in how the other three men stare at me like I'm something to be devoured.

This is beyond my most fevered imagination. The feminist in me should be appalled at being objectified like this, but my body thrums in anticipation. The part of me that had to endure Declan's insults is thrilled to capture the attention of four powerful men.

"On the bed." Mr. Macan gives me a gentle push, and I climb on the mattress on my hands and knees.

"That's it," he says. "Now, show them your pussy."

I part my thighs and plant them firmly into the mattress, then bend my spine in a graceful arch. My hips rise toward the canopy of the four-poster, laying myself bare.

One of the men growls, the sound going straight to my clit.

"Are you wet from sucking my cock," Mr. Macan asks, "Or is it the fact that I and all my friends want to fuck you?"

"Both," I whisper.

This scene is hot, but knowing that Mr. Macan accepts me, wants me, and is prepared to play out my fantasies is the biggest turn-on of all.

His large hands clasp my hips, his thumbs sliding dangerously close to my asshole and stretching it taught. My stomach flips, not just because he's so close to my anus but because Mr. White appears on the other side of the bed, holding his thick cock.

Mr. Macan leans over my back and growls into

my ear, "I'm going to fuck you raw. Fill that tight little pussy with my cum."

His words slide across my skin like caresses, and my eyelids flutter closed. "Please."

"She's practically begging for cock," Mr. White says.

"Look but no touching," Mr. Macan growls, his voice as hard as steel.

My eyes snap open, and it's to find Mr. White still in position.

"Of course," he says.

Liam stands behind the four-poster's low headboard, his arm moving up and down, while the third gentleman, whose name I think is Callum, stands at the foot of the bed.

Mr. Macan slides his cock up and down my wet slit, making sure to linger on my clit. I drop my head and moan into the mattress, my body trembling.

"Tell my friends how much you want this cock," he growls.

"P-please." I can barely stutter the words. "I need it. I need you to fuck me senseless in front of your friends."

He pushes in, his thick cock stretching me open, inch by delicious inch. Pleasure races up and down my core, and I cry out. I've used some heavyweight dildoes in my time, but his girth makes it feel like I've never truly been fucked. He fills me so completely that I swear I can feel him in the back of my throat.

Sensation floods my pussy, stretching up my belly and down to my toes. Mr. Macan presses all the way inside, so his stomach lies flush against my back, his balls brushing my inner thighs

"Oh, God," I moan.

"That's right, darling," he growls. "And you're going to cry out in exaltation."

The pulse behind my clit pounds like a marching drum, and my walls flutter in double time around his length. It's impossible to adjust, especially when he's buried himself to the hilt, and every muscle in my core is stretched to its limit.

When Mr. Macan cups my breast, making Mr. White moan.

"She's got such beautiful tits," the other man says.

I've been so focused on Mr. Macan's huge cock that I almost forgot about the gentlemen surrounding the bed. My gaze snaps up to find Mr. White stroking his cock with slow, deliberate caresses. Precum beads from its tip, only to fall on the silk sheets.

"She does, doesn't she," Mr. Macan says with a growl. "But her cunt is even sweeter."

Mr. White. "You bastard. I was going to ask Miss

Demeanor for a private dance, but you beat me to it."

I bite down on my bottom lip to hide a smirk. From the grumblings of the other men around the bed, it sounds like they also want to fuck me, too.

"Is she milking you, Angus?" Liam asks.

"She's tighter than a fist," Mr. Macan says.

My muscles spasm around his cock, making him groan.

Mr. Macan's other hand grips my hip as he pulls back. I suck in a sharp breath, already missing his girth. Then he pauses, his thick cockhead stretching my entrance.

Anticipation makes my stomach dip. It's like jumping off a high dive board or plunging on a roller coaster. I know what's coming, but I don't know what to expect.

His lips brush against my neck, sending shivers up and down my spine.

"Ready?" he asks.

I nod, my pussy clenching. Ready would be an understatement.

He snaps his hips forward, driving in so deeply that sensation explodes across my core. It's so intense that I scream.

My fingers twine around the sheets as he rams into me from behind, his cock hitting me deep with each stroke. His hands grip my hips so tightly that I'm sure he's leaving bruises. My breasts jiggle with each hard thrust, and my eyes roll toward the back of my head.

I glance to my right to find Callum reaching into his pants. Like my soon-to-be-ex fiancé, he's a strawberry blond but with mature, masculine features instead of Declan's boyish face. But none of the gentlemen pleasuring themselves around the bed can compare to Mr. Macan.

Heat radiates from my core, building so quickly that I'm already close to exploding. I grind my hips back against Mr. Macan, deepening the sensations.

"So fucking sexy," Liam growls.

"She can't get enough," Mr. White says with a moan, his hand speeding up around his cock.

He's right. I never want this moment to end. Not just because Mr. Macan is driving me toward a powerful orgasm, but because I've never felt so desired. This is more exhilarating than performing onstage.

Still balls-deep inside me, Mr. Macan pulls us up to a position where I'm sitting on his lap and he's thrusting into me from behind. He adjusts my thighs, so everyone can see where his cock enters my pussy, but most importantly my swollen, red clit.

Mr. White gapes, his mouth falling slack, his gaze roving up and down my naked form.

Liam groans.

"So hot and wet," Callum says, his hand moving a little faster.

"Fuck," he growls. "She's so goddamn gorgeous. Watching her makes me want to join in."

Mr. Macan's growl reverberates across my back. I can't see what he's doing with his face, but Mr. White raises a palm and smirks as though passing off his words as a joke.

It looked like he was deadly serious.

Sharp teeth clamp down on my earlobe, sending a shock of pain that goes straight to my clit. "Come on, sweetheart," Mr. Macan growls, his hips grinding into me with circular motions. "Be a good girl and show these lucky gentlemen how you cum."

His large hands encircle my elbows and lift me a few inches. Oh, fuck. I think he wants me to ride his cock.

This position is new to me—reverse cowgirl, but we're sitting up. I raise my hips as much as I can before sliding down his cock. Somehow, being in control of the movement is more intense because I can lean forward and adjust the position.

When I find an angle that allows Mr. Macan's cock to hit a sensitive spot, I continue with it until

I'm panting and moaning. All the gentlemen groan, in appreciation and also perhaps a little envy.

Pleasure licks at me like flames, detonating a display of fireworks behind my eyes. I squeeze them shut and focus on my approaching climax.

"Look at me," Mr. White rasps. "Please."

My eyes snap open, and I find Mr. White gripping his cock so tightly that its head turns purple. It looks like he's trying to stop himself from cumming.

The intensity of his gaze infuses every corner of my being with pleasant tingles. Desire etches his features, and it's all for me. Knowing how much he wants me makes my pussy close around Mr. Macan's thick shaft.

That's all it takes to push me over the edge.

Pleasure races through my system like an out-of-control fire. I jerk and moan against Mr. Macan's hard body, each flame intensifying as my orgasm reaches its peak. His strong arm wraps around my waist, holding me in place, while his other hand grips my hips.

"Look at you," he murmurs into my ear. "Cumming around my cock in front of all my friends. Such a good girl."

His words stoke the flames of my climax, and my pussy clamps around his cock, making him hiss through his teeth.

"So wet, so tight, so mine," he growls.

"Yours," I cry out, my gaze still fixed on Mr. White whose chest rises and falls like bellows.

Maybe it's the presence of three men devouring me with their eyes, but this is the most powerful orgasm of my life—even more intense than the one I had after the spanking.

My muscles continue to clench and spasm, as though trying to milk Mr. Macan of his cum, but he holds tight, his heart a heavy beat against my back.

"Fuck," says Mr. White, his hand dancing over his thick cock. "I can't hold back much longer."

"I don't need to remind you of our code of conduct," Mr. Macan says, his voice threatening.

Before I can consider what that means, Mr. White twists to the side, letting out a stream of pearlescent cum. He moans and thrusts through his climax, his eyes fixed on mine.

Leaning against Mr. Macan's back, I ride through the rest of my orgasm, my pussy clenching and spasming around his erection. Mr. White's spurts die down, and he bends over double, his breath coming in rapid pants.

"Miss Demeanor," Callum says, his voice strained. "Please."

I turn my head to the right to find the blond man staring into my eyes before he climaxes in one huge burst. Creamy white cum dribbles down his fingers as he jerks himself to a shuddering orgasm.

When he finishes, he gazes at me, his green eyes sparkling. "You're very beautiful."

"Thanks," I say with a lazy smile.

Liam's loud groan fills the room. My gaze snaps to the left, where he's holding onto the headboard, barely able to stand.

"Please, touch those lovely tits."

Before I can raise my hands to my breasts, Mr. Macan's thick fingers are already stretching and rolling my nipples.

"Like that?" he asks.

"Fuck. They're glorious."

Mr. Macan chuckles. "Every part of Miss Demeanor is glorious."

My chest flutters, even though I know it's silly to be so flattered. But what's truly silly is falling prey to Declan's insults. Nothing that little bastard could ever say will detract from how these gentlemen make me feel.

"Well done, Miss Demeanor," Mr. Macan murmurs. "It's time to say goodbye to my friends."

I raise a hand and give them each a wave. Mr. White blows me a kiss and makes the 'call me' gesture with his hand. Smiling back, I shake my head. This is just a one-off.

Mr. Macan peppers my neck with kisses, his large hands roaming over my skin. I expect him to shove me down and drive into me until he cums, but he cups my chin.

"I'm going to fuck you against the window, so the whole club can watch you cum. Objections?"

Chapter Fourteen

No objections. None, whatsoever. There's no way I'll miss another round of sex with Mr. Macan, let alone another chance of performing in front of a bigger audience.

He pulls out, leaving me clenching and empty, even though I'm still trembling from the aftershocks of my orgasm.

"Did you see how much my friends wanted you?" he murmurs.

"Yes," I whisper. "The one wearing white even gave me his card."

He turns me around so we're kneeling face to face, and places his hands on my shoulders. "You're not calling him."

"I already told him this was a one-off."

"Good, because you're mine."

My breath catches. Somewhere in the deep recesses of my mind, I thought he would judge me for the public sex, even though it was his idea. It's the kind of bullshit Declan would pull.

But he still hasn't cum. Everything might change once his mind is clear of lust.

"Who do you belong to, Aileen?"

"You," I murmur. "I belong to Angus Macan."

"Say that again."

"I belong to Angus—"

"My name," he says.

"Angus," I whisper.

His lips crash on mine in a kiss that's so possessive and fierce that my heart turns a somersault. His tongue pushes into the seam of my lips and twines around mine with delicious strokes. My pussy throbs in unison with my frantic heart. I can't get enough of his taste.

"From now on, call me Angus," he groans into the kiss.

"Angus."

He wraps my arms around my waist and shoulders then pulls me into his hard chest. His erection presses into my body. It's warm and still wet with my juices. I reach between our bodies, trying to stroke his cock, but he grabs my hand.

"No, sweetheart. You need to wait."

I gaze into his darkened eyes.

"When I cum, it's going to be deep inside your sweet cunt."

"Promise?" I ask.

"I guarantee it. Your only choice is whether you want it in this bed or by the glass in front of the entire club."

My pussy clenches with a fresh surge of arousal. I don't even need to think about his proposal. "How's it going to work?"

After kissing me on the lips, he gets off the bed and picks up his phone. My gaze tracks his glistening erection that bobs with each step. I can't believe one man can have so much self-control.

"I can text the MC to direct the audience's attention to the viewing room," he says. "The seats swivel in all directions, so everyone can get a good view of the action."

"Wow," I whisper.

"So?" he asks, his brow raised.

I bounce on the mattress. "Do it."

He flashes me a grin.

After a few exchanges of text messages, we wait for the current act to finish. Mr. Macan walks to a wooden cabinet and picks up a glass.

The muscles on his back and ass flex and relax in

time with his movements. His perfection is so distracting that it barely registers when he asks, "What do you like to drink?"

I raise my shoulders. "Something without alcohol, please."

"You don't drink?"

"I never got a taste for it."

He opens the cabinet door to reveal a refrigerator. "Brains, beauty, intelligence, and kink. How can one girl be so perfect?"

I dip my head, hoping he'll mean every word afterward. Some men are so convincing when they're seducing women, but turn into bastards the moment the cum has cooled.

He returns with two cans, and he offers me the coke. "Something on your mind, Aileen?"

Shit. I don't want to scare him away by sounding needy, but I'm also curious about this arrangement he has with the other voyeurs.

I take the coke, pull on its ring, and scramble for the right words. "You do this every week?"

"Are you asking if I bring a different woman here to parade in front of my friends or if I come here every week to watch and wank?"

He sets his can on the bedside table, lowers himself onto the mattress, and takes my hand. "I only come here when Sean nags me about being

DANCE FOR DADDY

single. He's brought performers here before and has allowed me and a few others to watch."

"Sean?" I ask.

His lips curl into a smile. "Was he so unmemorable you forgot his name? Sean's the asshole in the white tuxedo."

"Oh."

I bring the Coke to my lips and take several long gulps, trying to buy time to muster up the courage to speak. "Won't you think less of me for tonight?"

He takes my can, sets it aside, and grips my shoulder. "If you'd gone to Sean's room for a private dance, would you have let him talk you into anything more?"

I shake my head. "Absolutely not."

He nods, as though confirming something he already knows. "I have a question for you."

"What is it?"

"Are you going along with my suggestions because you want to, or am I a way to avoid marrying Declan?"

My jaw drops. "Of course, not. No. I said no because I felt comfortable with you and because..."

He leans closer. "Because?"

I can't believe he wants me to spell it out, but I need to return the favor, considering how much he's boosted my confidence. Those men might have called me beautiful because of the wig and makeup, but Angus hand-picked me out of dozens of girls to marry his son. Knowing that he did it because he admired my other qualities is the biggest compliment.

"You're really attractive," I murmur. "And you've got this imposing presence. When you look at me, I can't help but feel appreciated and beautiful. You make it safe to be myself."

His blue eyes twinkle. "Did you find me attractive before tonight?"

"You were always too intimidating. I only knew you by reputation and couldn't look you in the eye."

"And now?"

"You're much kinder than I expected, and I love the way you're letting me play out my fantasies.

"When our engagement is official, you can dance as much as you want, but only in disguise and when I'm there to protect you."

My heart flips. "When you asked me to be yours, I thought—"

"You'd become my mistress?"

I nod.

"I swore to myself that I wouldn't sleep with another woman unless she was the one I wanted to become my wife."

My eyes flutter shut, and I exhale the longest

breath of relief. Declan said something similar except he accused Angus of being gay. If I'm the one he chose to sleep with, then he wants us to have a future.

"Are you alright?" he asks.

"I thought you'd change your mind about me after tonight," I blurt, my insides twisting at being so vulnerable.

He cups the side of my face. "Aileen, look at me." When I peer up at him through my lashes, he continues. "I'm as open-minded as the next guy, but I don't do casual sex. You are stuck with me, for better or for worse."

Warmth fills my chest, and the backs of my eyes begin to sting. All thoughts of him changing his mind about me and breaking the agreement vanishes, replaced with the excitement of a life with Angus.

"Gentlemen, we have a special treat," a voice pipes through the speaker. "Please welcome the return of Miss Demeanor. She's agreed to perform a very special dance in the observation room."

Chapter Fifteen

A thunderous applause pipes through the speakers, making my heart pound harder than it did the last time I was onstage. Only this time, there's a second set of thrumming in my clit.

Angus opens a drawer on the bedside table and pulls out a mask that covers the top half of his face. Then he adjusts my mask and wig before helping me off the bed. He's just as naked as I am with his erection standing flush against his abs. I still can't believe this man's self-discipline. Still can't believe that of all the women he could have chosen, he picked me.

We walk hand in hand toward the wall of windows, which are now brightly illuminated by a row of ceiling spotlights I hadn't noticed until now.

My throat dries, and I gulp hard, my legs starting to falter.

Angus gazes down at me with his brows raised. "Are you alright?"

I place a hand on my stomach. "Butterflies."

"That's all?" he asks. "Because if you've changed your mind—"

"I haven't," I blurt.

I think I have an exhibitionism kink. Performing to an appreciative audience is more than a quick way to counterbalance every indignity I faced during my shitty engagement. Having a fiancé who wants me as much as I want him is beyond my wildest dreams.

He grins down at me, his eyes darkening. "Good, because I'm going to fuck you against that window until you come apart around my cock. Then and only then, will I fill that tight little cunt with cum."

His filthy words send a fresh wave of desire rolling through my insides, and my pussy clenches with need. Seeing the effect I have on him is a heady rush.

We reach the window to find the stage dark, the only lights below coming from the bar and the occasional strike of a lighter. Then images of us appear on a projector, making my heart skip.

That explains why Angus adjusted my mask and wig—to protect my identity.

Angus leans into me and whispers, "Be careful, Miss Demeanor, microphones at the window will broadcast anything you say to the stage."

I nod, my gaze returning to the stage lights.

Saxophone music plays through the speakers, drowning out the applause. I lick my lips, roll my shoulders and hips to the tune, and wait for Angus to make the first move.

He moves in behind me, his hands on my waist, his thick erection pressing into my lower back. He slides his palm up my ribcage and cups my breast.

My pussy tightens at the sight of us on the projector screen, and I breathe hard through parted lips. If performing in front of an audience was exciting, watching myself with Angus is decadent.

I continue swaying, my insides shivering at the touch of his skin. This is like stepping into an erotic dream, only this one guarantees an orgasm.

He rolls my nipple between his fingers, making me throw my head back against his shoulder.

"You like it when I play with your tits, Miss Demeanor?" he asks.

"Yes," I whisper.

"Does it make you wet?"

"Yes, sir."

He pulls my nipple hard, making me moan, and trails kisses down my neck and over my shoulder.

"Let's see if you were exaggerating about being wet." He slips his hand down my front, his fingers sliding over my pubes and through my folds.

My clit pulses at his touch but he doesn't linger, instead pressing a finger into my opening.

"I knew it," he says. "You're dripping wet."

"Aaah," I say.

"Lift your leg," he says. "Show the gentlemen that sweet, little pussy."

I do as ordered, balancing my weight on one foot, while Angus hooks his forearm under my hamstring. Cool air travels over my bare sex, making me feel even more exposed.

"Good girl." He slips two fingers inside. "So tight, Miss Demeanor."

"Th-thank you."

"I love how your pussy lips spread for me. Just for being so obedient, I'm going to give you a choice. What will it be: my fingers or my cock?"

"Cock," I say. "Please."

He chuckles.

"Lean against the window. Show the gentlemen downstairs how much you want it."

I lean a shoulder on the glass and fix my gaze on the curvaceous blonde on the projector. Her movements are graceful, her body a perfect hourglass. I can't believe that this person is me.

DANCE FOR DADDY

Even when Angus compared me to a young Elizabeth Taylor, I thought it was just an empty compliment, but he had meant every word. The woman in the projection radiates the confidence of a pin-up model.

Hell, everything Jennifer ever told me is true. I am beautiful. I have talent. I have poise. When she said all those things, I thought it was just a best friend trying to boost my ego. Now, I understand that she was telling me the truth.

I'm so mesmerized by the sight of us that it barely registers when Angus lines his cockhead at my entrance. But my little bubble of self-absorption vanishes when he enters me with one stroke.

Ecstasy surges through my veins as his thick shaft slides deep into my core and pushes against my cervix.

"Oh, fuck," I moan, reveling in being so full.

Getting fucked standing up is even more intense than having sex on a bed. The leg I'm standing on trembles, and my walls won't stop spasming around that delicious girth.

Intensity tilts my world on an axis, but I place a palm on the window to hold myself steady.

"What a greedy little cunt you have, Miss Demeanor," Angus says as he pounds into me, each thrust pushing my breasts against the cool glass.

"The way you clench around my cock is almost like you're trying to milk me of my cum."

All I can do in response is groan.

Angus fucks me with long, slow strokes, as though he's committing this moment to memory. I'm so sensitive that I feel every vein, every contour, every ridge of his huge cock.

"That's it, sweetheart. Show those men down there how much you love my cock."

I buck against him, as much as I can with my face pressed against the glass. Around the stage below us, I catch flickers of movement, but I'm so entranced by the sight of his muscular body behind mine that I lose interest in what's happening.

"Oh, god," I groan.

"He can't help you now, but my cock will take you to heaven." He snaps his hips, making me see stars.

I cry out, my vision going black. He isn't exaggerating. Anything is possible with this angle and his impressive girth. He's hitting spots inside me that no toy or fingers have ever reached.

"You feel so fucking good on my cock. I can feel you squeezing it like you're pumping me for cum."

My breath quickens, and I exhale a moan.

"You want to taste my cum, don't you, sweetheart?"

"Yes," I cry.

"Then tell me." He snaps his hips. "Tell me how much you want it. Beg me for my cum."

"Please," I whisper. "Give it to me."

"Louder."

"I want your cum," I cry out. "I want your cock."

"Good girl."

He thrusts into me deep and hard, making the leg I'm standing on buckle. Luckily for me, Angus is there to catch me before I fall. He lowers my other leg, sets them both on the floor, and pushes down my back.

I press my hands against the window, enjoying the coolness of the glass against my clammy palms. Angus fucks me from behind, his hips rocking a gentle rhythm. It's as though he's giving me a break from the strain of sex on one leg, but each stroke infuses me with a wave of molten pleasure.

My gaze darts toward the huge projector, where the blonde's breasts wobble and shake with every thrust. I'm sexy. Sultry. Seductive. Behind me, Angus looks glorious. His biceps bulge as he holds onto my hips, and his muscles bunch and release with his powerful thrusts.

This is more exciting than watching online porn

because I'm the star. Everything happening to the woman is happening to me.

I think I've found a new kink—one that combines exhibitionism but satisfies my need to be anonymous. The next time I have sex with Angus, it's going to be in front of a mirror.

Seeing myself like this pushes my pleasure to another level of intensity, and my clit aches with the need to be touched. Pressure builds up around my core and my entire body trembles with sweet tension.

Sweat breaks out across my palms, and I flatten them against the window. I'm so close to climaxing, but I don't want the feeling to end.

Angus's large palm slides over my ass cheek, and the pad of his thumb brushes against my pucker, sending a surge of sensation up my spine.

"Oh, fuck," I groan.

"I'm going to give you all the cum you can handle," he growls. "Would you like that, Miss Demeanor?"

"Please."

I want to close my eyes and focus on the kaleidoscope of sensations racing through my body, but my gaze is fixed on the screen. The blonde's features twist as though she can't decide if she's in agony or ecstasy.

Angus shifts our position once more, so I'm

standing with my body flush against the glass, my feet on his as he fucks me from behind. One of his hands grips both wrists and holds them over my head, while he slips the fingers of his other hand through my wet folds.

"Are you going to be a good girl for me and milk my cock?"

"Yes," I say from between clenched teeth.

"Full answer, Miss Demeanor," he growls. "Tell me exactly what you will do."

"I'm going to milk your cock, Sir."

He rewards me by rubbing my clit. I shudder, trapped between his larger body and the window, my arms restrained. I can't even move my legs because he's pressing them into the glass.

"What a swollen little clit," he says, his fingers closing around the sensitive bud. "So hard and responsive."

My eyes roll to the back of my head. "Oh, fuck."

"That's my girl. Keep pulling on my cock with your hungry little cunt."

He's so dirty. But I love it. I have to bite my lip to keep from crying out as he rolls my clit between his thumb and forefingers. The insides of my thighs are so wet with my juices that they're leaving a smear on the glass.

Angus pinches my clit, and something inside me

cracks, releasing a flood of liquid lightning. My orgasm hits my body like an electric shock, with jolts of pleasure making my limbs quiver and jerk. My soul goes into orbit, propelled by currents of sensation. The only thing keeping my body grounded is Angus's powerful frame.

"Just like that," he says, his voice a rumbling growl. "Squeeze my cock with your cunt, Miss Demeanor."

My muscles clench around his shaft, making it swell.

"You're so fucking beautiful when you're milking my cock."

As I tighten down on his cock, and the walls of my pussy spasm around his length, his strokes become erratic. Even in the throes of my most powerful orgasm, I feel his cock thicken inside me. My ear fills with a deep groan, and my pussy fills with hot cum.

I melt against the window, a puddle of satisfaction I feel deep in my soul. It's not just about the mind-blowing sex. It's the relief of letting go of the restraints of my former life and finding a man who not only wants me but has brought out a side of my personality that I didn't dare entertain.

Angus's strong arms gather me up, and I rest my head against his shoulder.

DANCE FOR DADDY

"You're mine," he murmurs as he carries me across the room. "Don't you ever forget."

Those reassuring words are all I need to let my eyes flutter shut and melt into his embrace.

Chapter Sixteen

E ven though I'm in a strange bed, I enjoy the deepest, most relaxing night of sleep for the first time since Dad's business went to shit, with dreams of me waltzing with Angus. We're in the ballroom of his mansion, surrounded by our combined families.

Everyone smiles and claps for us, but the music stops when the doors slam open. The crowd parts, and Declan storms into the room, flanked by a pair of tall blondes and his drug dealing friends at his back.

He points his finger and is about to speak when I jerk awake.

Sunlight streams in from a window at the far end of Angus's room at the club. I glance around, looking for signs of him, but all I find are my clothes, neatly piled on a chair.

My breath catches.

Angus is gone.

He probably came to his senses last night and decided I was too much trouble. That or he's still hung up on his long-dead wife and wants to remain a widower.

I push myself up, swing my legs out of the bed, and pad across the room to my clothes. Stacks of fifty-pound notes lie nestled in my open bag, a reminder of how much Angus paid for my services.

My heart sinks to my stomach and ties itself into a painful knot. A long sigh escapes my lips, and I squeeze my eyes shut. On the plus side, I have enough cash to help Jennifer and pay for somewhere else to stay. Even if Angus no longer wants me, I don't think he'll make me marry his son.

The backs of my eyes itch and the skin around them grows hot. I press my lips together and force back the tears. Last night was just a fantasy. A wonderful, erotic fantasy where I let down my guard and gave myself to a man who really wanted me. It was wonderful while it lasted.

When I pick up my leather top, a rectangular piece of paper floats to the table. It's Mr. White's business card. He must have slipped it in my clothes when I wasn't looking.

A smile curves my lips, and my chest warms with the feeling of being desired. But last night was a one-off. Ignoring the card, I pick up the rest of my clothes and walk to my bag.

"What are you doing?" A deep voice jolts me out of my musings.

I whirl around to find Angus standing in the doorway that leads to the bathroom. His arms are folded over his bare chest, and his sleep-mussed hair makes him look too good to be real.

My gaze wanders down to the towel draped around his hips and lingers on the way it tents with a growing bulge. "Um... I thought you'd left."

He strides across the room with such determined steps that I back toward the table.

"You're not getting away from me so easily." he bends down, hooks his arm beneath my knees, and lifts me off my feet. "At least not until you're wearing my ring."

The knot in my stomach loosens.

"So, you didn't change your mind?" The words tumble from my lips before I can stem the flow.

His steps falter, and he stares down at me with a crease in his brows. "What makes you think I wound't want you?"

"When I didn't see you on the other side of the bed, my brain started coming to all sorts of conclusions," I mutter. "Like maybe girls who have sex in public aren't marriage material."

Angus tightens his lips and carries me into a huge bathroom with marble tiles that reflect the light from the chandelier. A sunken tub large enough for four sits in the center of the room, brimming with bubbles. At the far end stands a low table with a bucket of champagne and two glasses, and a basket of croissants.

He sets me on my feet, and the towel slips down to reveal his thickening cock.

"Clearly, I still want you." He takes my hand and walks me to the edge of the bath. "I can't see that ever changing."

My heart stutters like a needle bouncing off a vinyl record, and my breath catches at his words. I can hardly blame myself for worrying. This time yesterday, I was going to marry a man I despised. Now, I have a man who fulfills my every need.

"Okay," I whisper.

"Okay?" His brows rise with expectation.

"I still want to marry you, too."

His features relax, and his mouth lifts into a smile, leaving me wondering if he ever had doubts about me changing my mind.

He wraps his arms around my shoulders and pulls me into his chest. "Good, because I've already called for a meeting with your father and my son."

My jaw hangs open with a gasp. "When?"

"Tonight."

Shock courses through my veins. I can barely process how quickly everything is happening. This feels like some kind of mafia fairytale, and I'm the heroine who's about to have her wishes come true.

"Aileen?" he asks, searching my face.

I blink the spots out of my vision and muster up a response.

"This is amazing," I say, my voice breathy with awe.

He frowns. "But?"

"Just wondering how Dad will take the news." I shake off that thought. "Not that it matters. He and Mum knew I was miserable with Declan, but they kept assuring me that things would be different after we were married."

Angus tightens his jaw. "Your father should want the best for you instead of letting you suffer."

I raise my shoulders and suppress a shudder at the thought of loan sharks, traffickers, or organ harvesters. "The alternative was worse."

His eyes soften, and he exhales his annoyance in a long sigh. "Sorry doesn't begin to express how much

I regret my decision to put you and Declan together."

Warmth fills my heart and spreads across my chest. He was the last to know that the engagement was unhappy, yet the first to apologize.

"There was no way you could have known he would be so cruel," I murmur.

"Then should I be angry that you never told me?" he asks, his arm wrapping around my waist.

"It's not like I could ever have access to a man like you," I murmur against his lips.

"You should know I would always make time for you."

I rock forward on the balls of my feet and peck him on the lips. "Thank you."

He brushes his thumb across my bottom lip. "I haven't begun to apologize, but I'll start by getting on my knees."

Now it's my turn to frown. The last thing I want is for Angus to beg, but I let him guide me to sit at the edge of the tub with my legs in the warm water. He steps inside, kneels down until the bubbles cover his chest, and places both hands on my knees.

My eyes widen. "Oh."

He runs the pads of his thumbs over the sensitive skin of my inner thighs, his gaze fixed on mine. "Let

DANCE FOR DADDY

me show you how sorry I am by making you feel good."

Heat spreads down my face and across my chest. My clit swells in anticipation of his touch.

"Please," I whisper.

He parts my legs and lands a trail of soft kisses up my inner thighs. Each touch of his lips sends tingles across my skin that race toward my clit.

I lean back, breathing hard through my parted lips and resting my weight on my hands.

Angus groans. "I've never seen a prettier sight than your bare pussy. I wonder if you taste as good as you look."

The muscles of my core clench. Fuck. I hadn't realized until now how much I love compliments and praise, and Angus is masterful with his words.

"Be a good girl and spread your lips for me."

With a gasp, I obey and lay myself bare. His gaze is heavy, and warm air swirls around my folds, making me groan.

Somehow, I feel even more exposed than I did yesterday when we fucked on the four-poster in front of his friends. Perhaps it's because I'm no longer playing the role of Miss Demeanor. There's no disguise to hide behind. I'm Aileen Walsh and he's Angus Macan.

Angus leans forward, his lips parted, his hot

breath fanning on my exposed flesh. He traces the tip of his tongue along my inner folds. I jerk forward, my spine lighting up with pleasure. He runs a slow circle around my clit that makes my legs tremble and then runs the flat of his tongue down to my opening.

"You taste divine," he whispers, "Just as I suspected."

I groan, my hips jerking.

Angus chuckles, his voice husky and low. "So eager, sweetheart? I'll take care of you. Just relax."

Hearing the words sets off a flock of happy butterflies. Angus isn't just about to look after my pleasure—he's looking after me. I will never have to struggle or worry about the future. I'm so blessed to have such an extraordinary man like Angus by my side—he's tender, thoughtful, and stunningly handsome.

"A-alright," I whisper and suck in a deep breath.

He teases my clit with slow, firm strokes that make my thighs quiver. I moan, my hand grabbing one of his shoulders. My back arches as his tongue glides down along my folds, slides to my opening, and travels back to my clit.

"Beautiful," he growls.

Pleasure courses down my thighs, and my toes curl. The way he alternates between pleasuring my clit and licking my folds keeps me deliciously off-balance.

My pussy throbs, still a little tender from accommodating his huge cock, but I'm too lost in the bliss of the moment to care. I need him to fill me with something, anything. I desperately need to cum.

"Please, Angus," I whimper, my nails digging into his shoulders.

"Please what?" he says, his voice low and deep. "Use your words."

As much as I want to say something seductive, my mind falls blank. I'm lost in pleasure, lost in lust.

"Fill me," I cry.

He chuckles. "You'll have to be more specific, sweetheart."

I groan, my hips jerking. "F-fingers."

"Someone's impatient," he says around my folds, his tone teasing.

"Please." My fingers fumble down his bicep as if I could ever reach his hand from this angle.

Still lavishing my clit with firm strokes, he circles my opening with his thick fingers. I bite down on my lip and swallow back a moan.

"Is this what you want, Aileen?" he asks.

My eyelids flutter shut. "Please."

"Eyes on me."

I glance down to find him staring up at me from between my legs, his gaze heavy with lust.

"Good girl."

A thrill races up and down my spine.

He presses two fingers at my entrance. "I want to hear you."

"Please," I say with a moan.

"Just like that."

He slides his finger into my pussy, triggering a deluge of pleasant shudders. I inhale a noisy gasp. His fingers pump in and out of me, building a steady rhythm in counterpoint to the delicious strokes on my clit.

Warm water cascades over my thighs and across the bathroom floor, but none of that matters. Not when Angus Macan is between my legs, giving me more pleasure than should be legal.

Nothing compares to the feeling of having a man who wants me as much as I want him. A man who cares deeply for my happiness. A man who takes charge. Each stroke of his tongue sends me to greater heights of ecstasy, and the pressure building up in my core teeters toward a breaking point.

My hips jerk and my eyes roll toward the back of my head.

"Oh god," I moan, my fingers reaching for his face. "I'm so close."

"That's it," he rumbles. "Cum for Daddy."

His words set off an avalanche of ecstasy. My muscles clench and release waves of sensation as I scream out an orgasm loud enough to shatter his eardrums. Every nerve ending comes alive, and it feels like the person I used to be is shattering into a million pieces.

"That's my girl," Angus says, his tongue slowing to prolong the orgasm and to put those pieces back together to form a new woman. I'm no longer the shy and self-conscious girl who took shit from her fiancé. I'm daring, desirable, and deserving. I'm the future Mrs. Aileen Macan.

Angus pulls me into the water, holding me through the aftershocks, his palms rubbing circles on my back. I rest my head against his shoulder, panting hard as he brings my consciousness back to reality.

"You were wonderful," he murmurs into my hair.

I'm too breathless to speak.

We hold each other until my breath slows, and my mind clears everything except Angus. I cling to his strong shoulders.

"Apology accepted," I whisper.

His deep chuckle warms my heart. "The apology has only just begun. How about breakfast?"

We settle in the tub with me on his lap, and he

calls room service to order a selection of dishes. We share long, leisurely kisses, until the doorbell rings.

Angus reaches between the taps and fires up a screen I hadn't noticed until now. A man in purple livery stands in the hallway with a tray of covered plates.

My stomach chooses that moment to rumble.

"Hungry?" he asks with a laugh.

"It's been a long, hard night," I reply.

Angus flips a switch that unlocks the door and lets in the man from room service. He turns back with a grin and scoops me back into his arms. I'm so lost in the kiss that I barely notice the door creak open.

"Dad?" says a familiar voice.

We draw back from the kiss to find Declan standing in the doorway, his mouth agape.

"Aileen?" he gasps.

Chapter Seventeen

Shock barrels through my insides, and I hiss through my teeth. I knew we'd have to face Declan today, but I didn't expect him to catch us in the act.

"Get out," Angus growls.

Declan remains in the doorway, still frozen in place with his mouth hanging open.

A tall blonde appears over his shoulder. "Is that your dad's new girlfriend?"

"Out," Angus roars.

My jaw clenches. Only this time I don't feel any sense of affront that Declan spent the night with yet another blonde model. I'm more furious for Angus. What kind of son walks in on his father when he's started a new relationship?

Flinching, the other woman drags Declan out of the doorway and lets the door swing shut.

Angus turns to me, his brow creased with concern. "I'm sorry, Aileen. I had no idea. Are you alright?"

"Fine." I smile. "I can't believe he could be so disrespectful."

A muscle tightens in his jaw. "I shouldn't have spoiled the boy, but that ends today."

My heart skips a beat. "What do you mean?"

"While I was running the bath, I did a little digging in the club accounts. Declan has run up quite a tab for the use of the recording room."

"That explains how he makes so many videos," I mutter.

"If my son wants to waste money on hotel rooms and models, he'll have to get a job."

Triumph flares in my gut, and I smile. "Yes. I've always thought Declan needed less money and more purpose."

Angus rises from the tub with water cascading down his muscular torso. It's strange how I don't give a shit that my fiancé just caught me cheating with his dad.

Every ounce of self-confidence I gained from last night floods back into my system, making my chest swell with pride. Declan dismissed burlesque dancing for stripping, yet it opened up an opportunity for love.

Angus helps me out of the tub and walks to the fluffy robes hanging behind the door.

My gaze follows his muscular ass, but when he picks up a robe for himself and one for me, my heart flutters.

I can't love Angus already, can I?

It's only been a few hours. He's everything I never dared to hope for in a romantic partner. Everything about him is attractive, including the fact that he's a high-ranking member of the mob. It's both protective and sexy.

"What are you smiling about, Aileen?" He holds open the robe, reminding me of the way gentlemen hold open ladies' coats in romantic movies.

"Nothing... I'm just happy." I slip my hands into the armholes and let him drape the robe over my shoulders. It's warm and soft, like being caressed by clouds.

When he wraps the belt around my waist, it's a cocoon of soft luxury. I gaze into his warm blue eyes and sigh as he tucks a strand of damp hair behind my ear. Any other man would be freaked out at being caught with his son's fiancée but Angus is more concerned with my comfort than with Declan's.

He leans down and kisses me on the tip of my nose. "I intend to keep you happy forever."

Anticipation skitters up my spine. "Forever sounds perfect."

We walk hand in hand through the bathroom door to find Declan sitting on a sofa, looking sullen and half the size he did yesterday. He must take after his mother because his frame has none of Angus's impressive bulk.

He glares up at us through razor-slitted brows but doesn't speak.

I can't believe this sulky brat is the same guy who pulled out a stack of fifties and goaded me into humiliating myself for money to get home.

His gaze sweeps up and down my robe-clad form, but he doesn't dare look at his father. I fold my arms across my chest, waiting for him to start spewing his usual insults.

"So that hot girl you fucked last night was her in a wig?" he asks.

My stomach twists at the thought of Declan seeing us on the screen.

"I don't remember giving you permission to discuss my sex life," Angus says, his voice cold.

Declan shrinks back into the sofa and scowls.

"Why did you do it, Aileen?" Declan says, his voice cracking. "Out of revenge?"

"We weren't exactly exclusive," I say.

His gaze snaps up to meet mine. "But you're my fiancée!"

Angus steps in front of me, blocking my view of Declan. "And a fat lot of good you did to make her happy," he snarls. "Cheating, insults, neglect—"

"I didn't—" Declan begins to say, but Angus cuts him off with a wave of his hand.

"Don't think I don't know about the shit you post on social media and your twice-weekly sessions in the club's recording room."

Declan's mouth clicks shut.

"Fine," he mutters and pulls himself to standing and glares in my general direction without looking me in the eye. "So, this makes us even. Get dressed, I'm taking you home."

"Aileen is no longer your fiancée."

Declan finally meets his father's eyes. "Shouldn't that be for her to decide—"

"I don't want you," I say.

Declan stiffens.

"Aileen has agreed to be with me," Angus says, his voice warm.

"You're joking," Declan blurts.

"Why would I want to stay engaged to someone so cruel?" I ask.

"You're just saying that out of spite." He nods for emphasis. "You can't want my dad. He's forty-four years old, and he's killed people—"

"Declan," Angus barks.

He flinches. "Sorry."

"There will be no more easy access to money," Angus says. "You will either get a job or enroll at Marina University."

I turn to Angus and smile. I've heard of Marina Uni. It's a place where high-ranking members of crime families send their children to learn subjects like finance, economics, and marketing. It's like getting a mafia MBA.

Declan huffs and stomps toward the door. "I'll go then, but don't come crying to me when she gains weight and turns back into a fat little four-eyed snob."

Irritation burns across my skin. I'm about to tell him that I'm the same fat little snob from yesterday morning and the same fat little snob he also said was hot the night before, but Angus descends on Declan like a demon and shoves him against the wall.

"You will address my future wife with respect," Angus snarls.

My heart skips a beat.

"Wife?" Declan stutters.

I pull my shoulders back and raise my chin, remembering every slight, every insult he dished out in the past year.

"That's right," I say with a smirk. "I might not have been able to influence you as your fiancée but I'm going to whip you into shape as your stepmother."

As Declan slinks out of the room, I send him a silent word of thanks. If he hadn't used his money to humiliate and debase me for fun, I would have danced onstage as Miss Demeanor to help Jennifer and gone straight home. I would have refused Mr. Burgundy's offer of a private dance.

But as they say, don't let your fiancé get in the way of marrying his dad.

Epilogue

Three months later.

Angus opens the limousine door, letting in the distant strains of orchestra music. He steps out, clad in a burgundy morning suit so dark that it almost appears black. He's even more handsome than he was when I spotted him in the gentlemen's club, with his eyes bluer and his jaw even more chiseled.

"Ready, Mrs. Macan?" He offers me a hand.

A flock of butterflies erupts in my stomach. This is the best summer ever. Not only did I get a first-class degree in English Lit, but I can't believe we're married. By the time Angus and I went to Mum and Dad's house to break the news of our engagement, Declan had already told them his version of the truth.

He painted me as a cheating gold digger who seduced a grieving widower and brainwashed him for financial gain. Declan also spread rumors that I was gang-banged by four men, including his father.

My parents were furious, saying that I had disgraced them and brought shame to the family, but Angus defended my honor and revealed that Declan had been abusive. Desperation made them blind to Declan's faults when we were engaged, and they were too stuck in their ignorance to see the truth. It took Mum and Dad a few minutes of scrolling through Declan's social media accounts to believe our side of the story.

They still disapprove of my marriage. Mostly because Angus is much older, runs an entire section of the mob, and is infamous for wiping out the entire Fian gang. They even tried telling me that my life would be in danger because Angus's first wife was murdered.

Mum and Dad conveniently forget to acknowledge that Angus slaughtered those people because they dared to touch his wife. His power has grown exponentially in the past decades, as has his reputation.

It's funny how they didn't fret so much for my well being when my previous relationship was abusive. I'm safer as the wife of a boss than the wife of a brat.

I no longer care so much about what they think.

Gathering up the voluminous skirt of my wedding dress, I extend my hand to Angus. He helps me out of the limousine and onto the white carpet stretching across the lawn to a huge, white marquee.

It's breathtaking, with ivory ribbons and gauzy curtains draping from a ceiling dotted with fairy lights. Waiting staff wearing white shirts and black bow ties stand at the marquee's entrance holding trays laden with champagne glasses.

My legs still tremble from the aftershocks of my last orgasm, and my chest swells with giddiness. I can't tell if I'm Cinderella or the duckling who discovered she was a swan.

Angus steadies me with an arm around my waist and pulls me into his side. He insisted on spending the twenty-minute ride from the cathedral to his mansion on his knees, spreading my thighs and eating my pussy until I squirted.

He gazes down at me, his eyes twinkling. "Satisfied, Mrs. Macan?"

"Ecstatic," I reply, unable to hide my smile.

"Have I told you how beautiful you look?"

A giggle bursts from my chest. "Only about a dozen times."

He leans down to give me a kiss, and I can taste myself on his lips. Heat rushes to my cheeks. I reach into the bodice of my dress, extract a handkerchief, and dab his mouth.

Angus smirks. "Taste something you like?"

"That's not funny." I rub harder. "You can't walk around the reception, tasting like my pussy."

Chuckling, he draws back and bats me on the nose. "I'll be as good as new with a few swigs of champagne."

"There you are!" Our wedding planner, a tall red-haired woman wearing a teal suit, sprints alongside the white carpet, clutching a clipboard. "Didn't you get any of my messages? Security wants to know what to do with your son."

My lips tighten.

Declan took the news the worst. When nobody believed his gang banging story, he ran to everyone who would listen and told them I fucked Angus in front of an entire nightclub. Declan's older brothers thought the story was hilarious if untrue. Everyone else dismissed it as his usual bullshit until Declan told his grandfather—the leader of the Irish mob.

The old man somehow obtained some grainy footage someone took from the projector and demanded that Angus clean up his reputation and marry me within the next three months. Declan's plan to break us up backfired, and Angus sent him to Marina University.

Now, he's training to become a mafia accountant.

Declan refused to attend the wedding, claiming that he was in love with me all along but was afraid to express his feelings. He's just pissed off that Angus finally made him grow up and kicked him off the gravy train.

"What's happened?" Angus asks the wedding planner.

"He arrived with a rowdy group of companions," the woman replies.

She means Ali and the other dealers. I'm surprised they're still friends, considering Declan no longer has the cash to flash. Angus loads up Declan's university credit so he can pay for groceries, laundry, and coffee, but he's not allowed off campus.

"Where is he now?" I ask.

The planner leads us across the lawn to a portable structure guarded by four huge men wearing black and explains that the other members of Declan's group agreed to leave the moment they were challenged by security.

Angus turns to me and frowns. "Are you sure you want to be here for this?"

I take his hand. "We're family now. Your problems are mine, and I want to resolve this thing with Declan as much as you do."

The more I get to know Angus, the more compassion I feel for his situation. He blames himself for the death of his wife since the only reason she was murdered was because of a business rival. The guilt he suffered for his youngest son growing up without a mother figure has led to Declan becoming spoiled.

We both did couples and individual therapy because Angus wanted to become the husband I deserve, and with the help of my counselor, I've forgiven Declan.

The security guards step aside, letting us into the building. My stomach tightens, and I expect Declan to rush at us, looking as disheveled and drug-addled as the day he did when Angus sent him away.

Instead, his hair is several shades darker, neatly cut, and he's dressed in a navy suit.

Declan rushes to his feet, his gaze meeting mine for a second before sweeping down my gown. It's a boned bodice, constructed in similar lines to the corset I wore as Miss Demeanor, except with Swarovski crystals. The train and skirt, of course, are detachable.

I stand straighter, waiting for a snarky remark, but Declan licks his lips. "You look really beautiful."

His words float over me like a breeze. It's hard to take my new stepson seriously at times, but I'll make an effort for my husband.

"Why are you here?" Angus asks.

Declan raises his shoulders. "I came to say sorry for trying to get Aileen in trouble with grandad."

My lips tighten. From the way the planner spoke, it sounded like Declan came to cause a scene but only failed because of the security guards. Angus has made several attempts to reach him, but Declan prefers to speak to him through his older brothers. I have no idea what's going on in his tiny mind.

"Why don't you apologize to Aileen," Angus says.

Declan's eyes dart toward mine before dropping to the floor. "Yeah." He runs a hand through his hair. "Sorry about that. I've had time to think about it, and I was being a dick."

Any resentment I once had toward him is long gone, but that doesn't mean I believe his apology is sincere. I'm also not going to spoil my happiest day bickering with Declan.

"No harm done," I murmur. "It meant pushing the wedding forward and hiring a planner so I could concentrate on my finals."

"Exams go okay?" he asks.

"As well as they could with all the wedding

preparations." I might have had help, but I still had dress fittings, rehearsals, and a bachelorette party. "How's university?"

"I have a girlfriend. She's gorgeous," Declan blurts.

He searches my face for a reaction but only finds a bland smile. I was never jealous of his other women because I never loved him and never felt that he was mine. What I objected to were the constant comparisons, insults, and degradation.

Angus chuckles. "You should have brought her as your plus one."

Declan drops his gaze and rubs the back of his neck, making me suspect his new relationship is an exaggeration. "Yeah, well... It's early days."

My gaze wanders to the window, where a few stragglers pause at the marquee's entrance to take a champagne flute.

"Would you like to join the reception?" I ask. "Someone can make up a place setting at your brothers' table."

Declan blows out a breath that lifts his bangs. "Thanks."

"Behave yourself," Angus says.

He nods.

Angus sweeps out an arm toward the door, letting Declan leave first. As soon as it swings shut behind him, Angus wraps his arms around my shoulders and pulls me into a hug.

"Thank you for being so gracious," he whispers into my hair.

I wrap my arms around his waist. "We might have our differences, but Declan is still family."

He draws back and kisses me on the lips. "Every moment we spend together, my love for you grows a little bit deeper."

My heart swells until I'm overflowing with joy. "I love you, too."

Read the next book in the series, Dinner with Daddy

My ex's lover tried to kill me. Then my night *really* got interesting...

All I wanted when I got home was a warm bed. Well, I found one.

Too bad my fiancé and his stepmother were already in it.

They had a plan to get rid of his father. And they wanted my help—or else.

Fortunately, my brain worked fast enough to get me out of there. But I think it was fate that made me run into Bard Dearg, the sexy older man my ex planned to murder.

I was shocked when Bard swore to protect me.

Even more so when he took me to dinner with some *very* scary people. Then I was *gobsmacked* when he told me what he wanted.

See, I never thought I'd end up having the best sex of my life with a mafia daddy.

But I did.

Now, I'm surprising even myself with how eager I am to give him *everything* he wants, including revenge on his son.

And his new heir...

DINNER WITH DADDY

About the Author

I write dark contemporary and paranormal romance featuring villains, monsters, morally gray heroes, and the women who make them feral.

When I'm not writing steamy scenes, you'll probably find me at my TikTok, @SiggyShadeAuthor

Join my newsletter for exclusive short stories and updates on upcoming books: www.siggyshade.com/newsletter

Also by Siggy Shade

Contemporary Romance

Manacled to Medicine

Dinner with Daddy

Paranormal Romance

Tentacle Entanglement

Stalked by the Boogie Man

Jack's Head

Birched by the Krampus

Breeding with Bigfoot

Swallowing Water

Printed in Great Britain
by Amazon